The Lion's Brood

The Story of Hannibal

By
Rafael Scott

© 2010 by Rafael Scott

All rights reserved. No part of this book may be reproduced, stored in a retrieval system or transmitted in any form or by any means without the prior written permission of the publishers, except by a reviewer who may quote brief passages in a review to be printed in a newspaper, magazine or journal.

First printing, second edition

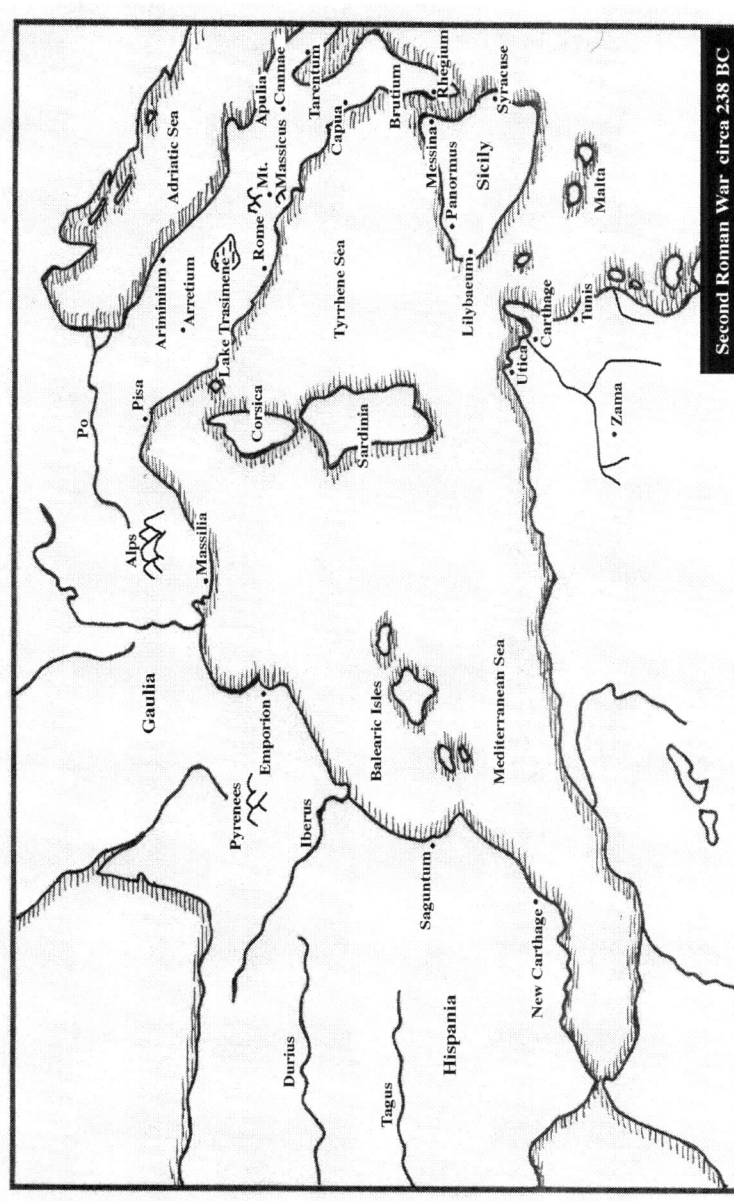

Prologue

Still a nine-year-old child, Hannibal slogged his way across the waist-high river of blood in the pitch black of night. The lion stood among the trees on the other side of the river, tracking his every move. Hannibal almost lost his balance a few times before succumbing to the slippery surface below and descending into the choppy, crimson waters. As he plummeted toward the murky bottom of the riverbed, he tried to hold his breath and swim upward—but to no avail. He eventually reached an underwater precipice and slipped off its edge. The gushing waters filled his mouth, choking him. Hannibal was drowning. His thoughts began to grow dim, and the dark waters blurred before him. Panicked, Hannibal had at first cried out. But then he felt no pain. His neck and limbs became lifeless, and he surrendered to his fate.

It was an unknown force that propelled Hannibal's small frame upward, lifting him to the surface. For a moment, he floated upon his back, drifting toward the closest shore. Hannibal could see his surroundings, yet he could not open his eyes. His chest heaved up and down, struggling to recapture precious air. Soon, young Hannibal regained his eyesight and once again waded across the turbulent river. Upon reaching the shore, he crawled up a muddy embankment, his hands digging into the earth, and his mouth gasping for air. He took a moment to catch his breath before lifting up his face, which, like his tunic, was heavily soiled with the ruddy mud of the river. There, directly within eyeshot, stood the lion, the nemesis that had haunted Hannibal for so many years.

The great, golden-mane beast waited for the boy on a small hill just above the shoreline. The animal rose from his powerful haunches and struck a pose that was evocative of the magnificent lion sculptures of ancient kingdoms. The glow of the moonlight bounced off the gushing river and into the lion's eyes. His pearly stare followed Hannibal up the incline. The lion grew uneasy and his roar brought Hannibal to a halt below him. A cold mist arose above the bloody river, leaving Hannibal drenched and shivering with fear. But he would not retreat. They must end. Eventually, they must come to an end.

"Why do you haunt me?" Hannibal screamed.

The lion replied with a thunderous roar, whose heavy wind enveloped the tormented child. Hannibal's teeth rattled as his arms dropped to his side. He countered his terror with fatalistic determination. "Why...do you haunt me?"

The lion opened his bone-crushing jaws and growled in discontent. His muscles rippled, but held still, ready to pounce. If the lion attacked, Hannibal wondered if he could make it to safety. Only a few meters separated the lifelong acquaintances, and all strength had abandoned the son of Carthage some time ago. Only time would tell.

1.

Bithynia, Asia Minor—182 B.C.

The dark and empty cobblestone streets of Bithynia, a city seated on the south coast of the Black Sea, gave way to a century of Roman legionnaires on horseback. Large steeds carrying thirty heavily armored soldiers slowly galloped through the splattering rain in twos. Their bronze helmets revealed only the piercing eyes of war-hardened Roman veterans. The young centurion leading the pack raised his palm to bring his men to an abrupt halt. Scanning the street lined with tattered inns and other rustic wooden dwellings, the narrow-framed officer arrogantly lowered his hand.

"Century, dismount!"

In unison, the legionnaires alighted and unsheathed their *gladi* from their scabbards. Holding the short swords in one hand, they removed the small, spearlike *pila* attached to their saddles.

"The consul states that he is here. So, we will find him. Disperse in threes and capture the Punic...alive!" the centurion said. Reluctantly, he looked over his shoulder to espy his superior mounted on horseback.

Consul Publius Cornelius Scipio gave his officer an approving nod. Scipio looked younger than his fifty years. He adjusted his crimson cape so that he could have a firmer grip on his *gladius*. Through his gold-hued helmet decorated with a crimson plume, he watched the detachment of legionnaires scatter in search of their prey. Scipio Africanus, as he was known on that day, wiped the strands of hazel hair from his steely eyes.

Unbeknownst to the Roman general and his horsemen, a scraggly haired, small, native boy hid in the darkness. The young lad in a soiled tunic, no more than nine years of age, dashed in a panic into the nearest two-story edifice. He scurried through a hidden, unhinged wooden panel that only his four-foot frame could squeeze past and made his way up the dark staircase.

"General! General! They are here!"

Hannibal Barca sat alone on a rickety chair before a small wooden table. With the exception of another old chair, some hay-filled bedding on the floor and a large wooden chest in the corner, there were no other furnishings in the damp room. The stout Hannibal's graying hair and beard contrasted sharply with his dark skin, which glittered in the candlelight. Dressed in a white toga, the aged man gazed at the scroll before him. A tear trickled down the crevices of his rugged skin as he viewed the contents of a scroll. This was what remained with him through the constant battles, the strife, the dying. He recalled the joy and playfulness he and his brothers shared in their youth and luxuriated in his bittersweet reveries, which commingled with the wine he sipped from a dull metal goblet. As Hannibal savored his drink, an uneasy calmness ran through his veins.

The boy from the street below barreled through the door. Amazed that the aging Carthaginian was not startled by his arrival, he stared at Hannibal in silence. Attempting to regain his breath from the sprint upstairs, he was afraid to utter another word until he could find the right ones.

Hannibal studied the youth with saddened eyes and

folded the scroll into his toga. Hannibal knew what the young warrior wanted to say before the boy could give the details. Hannibal rose from his seat and approached the youth, placing a warm hand on his head. "The Romans are here, are they?"

"Yes, General," the boy murmured.

"You are a good soldier, young friend." Hannibal gave the boy a reassuring smile. "Upon my horse, toward the back, there is a satchel filled with silver for you. A gift from Prusias."

The boy trembled, more from uncertainty than from the cold rains that were beating down outside. Yet he remained where he was, patiently waiting for Hannibal to relay a strategy for departure. "Shall I prepare your horse, General?"

"No," Hannibal replied in a tranquil tone. "You must leave now."

It had been two years since Hannibal had saved the boy from certain execution. King Prusias had ordered his entire family to be crucified after accusing them of collaborating to overthrow the ruler of Bithynia. Having gained favor with Prusias, Hannibal was able to convince the monarch to spare the boy's life but not his father, mother, and other siblings. Hannibal wondered what lived in the heart of a man who could willfully orphan a child on the strength of unfounded accusations whispered in dark corridors. Too many leaders believed these rumors, which could bring sorrowful consequences, he reflected.

The boy clenched the end of his tunic and the tears began to flow. "Is this what you said before, General? Is this the end?"

"Yes, Giscon. Yes it is. Go now."

Giscon wiped the tears, smearing them on his grimy face.

Giscon. That was his new name. It was not his birth name, but it was the one Hannibal used to refer to the fiery youth. The boy had grown fond of the name Giscon. He drew strength from it whenever it was uttered. And such resolve was precisely what was needed at the moment. Giscon placed his fist upon his small chest and quickly darted out the room.

With a single whisper of breath, Hannibal extinguished the candle.

The clamor of boot steps filled the murky hallway leading to Hannibal's room. Three legionnaires hunched their way toward the doorway, each quietly unsheathing his *gladius* and holding firmly to his *pilum*. They took their positions as they had been trained, one on either side of the door and one in front. The third legionnaire had a direct view of the room through the door, which was ajar about one meter. He was able to glimpse the empty chair that Hannibal had vacated and a corner of the wooden table. After clearing his eyes of the rain and cold sweat, he raised his *gladius* in anticipation of a sword attack.

The legionnaire kicked the door and it crept open, exposing the dim-lit space. The door creaked before drawing to a close. The soldier stood motionless. His eyes danced from side to side, awaiting a Carthaginian charge. It did not take long for the Roman to feel confident that there was no immediate danger. Comforted by the apparent emptiness of the room, he exhaled and shot his Roman comrades a reassuring glance.

Outside, two olive-skinned legionnaires knelt against a wall. A low, frightening whistle sounded, their only warning. Before either man could comprehend what was happening, they beheld their comrade pinned to the wall opposite them, a spear through his neck. The poor soul's feet dangled below, and blood gushed from his mouth as he tried to free himself. He gasped and cried out for them to help him, but they stood frozen, horrified. The two warriors watched as the man took his last breath, his head dropping to his chest.

The older of the two men turned to the other and whispered, "You hold him here while I summon the others."

The younger soldier had served in the legion after the end of the war with the Carthaginians. He had heard stories of the legendary battles pass from one elder to another in his home village of Arpi, but this was the first time he had ever witnessed death. He was breathing heavily and removed his helmet to get his bearings. "I'm not going in there alone!"

"He is an old man," the older Roman whispered.

"And I wish to be one someday!" The young soldier leaned against the wall, closing his eyes in prayer. "I am not going in there alone."

The older legionnaire lost patience and scurried over to the young man, bending down to avoid any further projectiles. He snatched him by the drenched collar of the crimson tunic under his plate mail and smashed the terrified soldier against the wall repeatedly. "We must inform the others! You are a Roman legionnaire! Go in there and restrain him. I will return with help very soon."

The young warrior nodded, regaining his composure. His more seasoned comrade pushed him away and crabbed his way to the other side of the doorway. Once past, he came to his feet, trotted down the hallway and faded into the shadows.

Donning his helmet, the young soldier closed his eyes and said a final prayer to Mars. Combat. This was not why he volunteered to join the legion. He only desired citizenship, silver to fill his clan's coffers and the prestige that accompanied it. He thought of the new bride he left behind in Etruria. Yet, courage, a fool's libation, entered his bloodstream and overpowered the very muscles holding his *gladius* and *pilum*. With one last deep inhalation, he slid his frame up the wall, poised for battle. Though his heartbeat increased to a rapid pummeling and every step he took was painstaking, he swallowed hard and entered the room. He was a legionnaire. Death was part of the greater glory of Rome. He would not be deemed a coward.

The chamber appeared empty, but he knew better. He had witnessed the javelin hurled from thin air just moments ago. "Where are you, Carthaginian?" His eyes darted from side to side and settled on the large weather-beaten chest. Spacious enough for a human being to easily crouch inside, he reflected. He pranced toward it in a stalking motion, weapons ready to strike. Once there, he readied himself for the unknown. He raised his sword and used the arrow tip of his *pilum* to pry open the lid. Before the chest contents were revealed, the sound of metal hitting the wooden floor behind him alarmed the young legionnaire, prompting him to twirl around and hurl his *pilum* at the source of the noise.

The spear embedded itself in the wall, and below it rocked back and forth the goblet that had fallen from the table. The young soldier's veins began to warm once more, no longer filled with the frozen uncertainty of death. As he stood there, a shadowy figure rose from the chest behind him. Hannibal placed the blade of his dagger around the neck of the legionnaire and tightened his hold on the young man's shoulder. He plunged the dagger with enough firmness to draw blood.

"Please do not kill me." The soldier pleaded for his life, unable to see his assailant's face.

"You hunt me like a dog. Release your weapon, Roman." The blade sliced deeper into the young man's throat.

The soldier did not blink; he lowered his *gladius* to his side. He had heard the countless stories of the deceptive Africans and was certain that once he dropped his blade, the Punic would slit his throat with extreme prejudice. He refused to fall victim to Punic trickery. If he were to die, it would be with honor that his wife would remember him. He reversed his *gladius* and fell backwards. He would not live to see the outcome. Hannibal attempted to avoid the strike and slashed the legionnaire's throat as he backed away. The aging warrior soon realized that his dexterity had failed him. The Roman's blade penetrated ,Hannibal's abdomen and his pallid toga was soon bathed in the blood that was escaping from his body.

Hannibal covered the wound with his bloody hand and watched the young legionnaire stare into his eyes from the floor below. The dying man tried to speak but was unable. His eyes sank into the back of his head and the gurgle ceased. He lay motionless in a pool of blood. Such a sight was not foreign to Hannibal. For many years, men at the height of their youth battled for power and supremacy of the Mediterranean. He recalled it all too well.

The furious Scipio marched down the hall, pushing the men stationed in the hall aside. He removed his helmet and let it fall to the floor. The intensity in his eyes was not to be denied. His graying hazel hair was short, yet flowing, wrapping itself around his statuesque olive brow. Even at his age, his muscles resonated through his tunic as he unsheathed his *gladius*. "What were my orders? What were my orders?!" he screamed.

Scipio reached Hannibal's closed door, forced it open and

pushed the centurion back. He glanced at the legionnaire being removed from the wall by other soldiers. "Remain here. I will go in alone."

The centurion took offense at being shoved by Scipio, in total disregard for protocol. But not wishing to risk charges of treason, he chose his words carefully. "Consul, it would not be--"

"Move aside!" Scipio elbowed his way to the door and quickly swatted it open. The men in the hall took defensive postures as Scipio entered alone.

Taking one step at a time, Scipio scanned the room for the presence of his long-time adversary. Yet he allowed his *gladius* to rest at his side, refusing to raise arms once again. "This is not befitting you, General. Hiding away like a coward." His eyes studied the dead legionnaire lying on the floor five feet away.

Scipio heard the door slam shut behind him. Before the anxious Roman soldiers outside could enter, the wooden slide lock was lowered, cutting Scipio off completely. The soldiers pummeled the door, attempting to free their commander as Scipio turned to face Hannibal Barca. For a moment, the old adversaries considered each other with knowing eyes. Hannibal held on tight to the wound, the blood was moving down his leg. With each trickle, Scipio became more concerned.

"One hides from what one fears. I hide from nothing." Hannibal conjured up what little energy he had left to finish the sentence. He stood firm in searing pain, his eyes never leaving Scipio's gaze. It had been ten years since Hannibal was able to speak with his formidable opponent. For years, Hannibal harbored unspeakable regret for allowing Rome's most accomplished military commander to live. It is the past that will haunt a man long before he reaches the heavens.

"I know." Scipio's expression of concern changed to the familiar enigmatic grin that had been so often returned by the man before him.

But at this moment, Hannibal was not smiling. "Why have you come?"

"Rome is bringing you up on charges. You are to be arrested and presented before the Senate for the crime of conspiracy to commit espionage."

Hannibal found such rhetoric amusing. He smirked at the notion. "Charges."

"I fail to see the humor, General."

"Tell me this, Scipio Africanus," Hannibal said sternly. "What of the crimes committed by Rome upon Carthage? Those are the charges that seem to have escaped the attention of your senate."

"You will receive a fair hearing. You have my word."

Hannibal grunted from the sharp pain in his belly. "Cato's word as well? You are naïve to your own people."

Scipio moved closer to Hannibal, glancing at the blood that was still flowing from his gash. "We both are naïve, General." He looked the wounded Hannibal straight in the eyes. "It was your Suffete who gave us your location."

"The Suffete." Hannibal gritted his teeth and staggered past Scipio, until he found a chair to rest upon. "They would leave a baby to drown if it meant more gold to fill their coffers." He sat and murmured in agony.

"Consul?" The muffled voice came from the other side of the barricaded door.

"Stand down. I am all right. The General and I shall be out shortly," shouted Scipio. The Roman consul faced Hannibal, more determined than ever to drag the

Carthaginian from the room if he had to. "It is time."

"I will not leave with you, Scipio." Hannibal reached for the goblet at his feet and filled it with wine from an old urn.

Scipio closed his eyes in frustration. "You or I have no choice." Scipio made his way to within a few feet of Hannibal.

"We all have choices, Consul," Hannibal said as he sipped the burgundy liquid, some of which trickled down his unkempt beard. "I made my choice long before you were born."

"Yes. A foolish promise of a boy to a bitter father!"

Hannibal responded in blind anger and raised his sword to within inches of Scipio's chest. "You know nothing!" The blade wagged before the Roman general's face.

"I am not your enemy." Scipio did not budge. His face relaxed into a kind, conciliatory mien.

"We were born enemies! War was inevitable!" Hannibal exclaimed as the wine splattered from his lips.

Scipio was now enraged. He slapped Hannibal's blade aside and rested his hands on the lopsided table, hovering over the wounded Carthaginian. "You started the war. It is you who has known only hate. It must end...the blood, the death. It must stop with us, Hannibal!" Scipio took a breath and regained his tranquil persona. "Follow me to Rome and plead your case."

The weight of the sword increased in Hannibal's mind and he no longer had the strength to hold it to the fire. The weapon fell and crashed to the floor. Hannibal rested his head in his free hand, rubbing his forehead for answers. "And what shall I plead for?"

"Defend your family name." Scipio believed in his ability to convince the Roman Senate to reconsider the order given to the senior co-consul.

Taken by the sincerity of Scipio's words, a smile escaped Hannibal's lips. Those words carried as much integrity as they once had in Africa. He remembered the days of battle where part of his soul perished with each engagement. It struck his heart as fast as the winds at sea that the man before him was his only connection to that day—the day he ceased to be the man he thought he would become. It started with Hanno. No, it began with the gloomy night before the altar of Ba'al beside Hamilcar, his father.

"Rome has already condemned me. But, you...no, I shall plead my case now, to you."

Scipio stepped away with caution. Though stunned at first by the Carthaginian's remark, he remembered that such a response was not out of character for Hannibal Barca. "I cannot be your counsel."

"You should be, for you know more than they ever could. But you must know all,"Hannibal added, "and I must tell someone I trust."

Scipio contemplated for a moment the request he had just received. He was torn. As a sworn Roman military commander, he had an obligation to Rome, *Senatus Populusque Romanus*. To barter with a Carthaginian was not only prohibited, it was outright treason, *perduellio,* punishable by death or something much worse—a life of condemnation. Yet his high regard for his former enemy ran deeper than mutual appreciation. In many ways, Scipio owed the man he was to the African who sat before him. There could only be one decision in the heart of the patrician.

"If I agree to be your counsel and hear you out, will you accompany me back to Rome?" Scipio embraced the opportunity to achieve a positive outcome, something he learned from Hannibal.

"I will return with you, without any malice." Hannibal panted and held tighter to the toga cloth covering his wound. "I swear before Ba'al."

"Then I shall listen." Scipio straddled the chair opposite Hannibal, waiting intently for the words to pour from the lips of the Carthaginian.

Hannibal swallowed another mouthful of wine and gazed over Scipio's shoulder as though creating a picture from memory and displaying it there in the distance. A powerful wave of pride pervaded his face.

"I think of the days of Carthage...my brothers. We too were naïve about our surroundings...and it was good. So peacefully
good." His eyes watered with remembrance, reaffirming the rarely acknowledged notion that old warriors hurt inside as well.

Carthage, Africa—238 B.C.

Power resonated from the northernmost point of the continent where Africa kissed the Mediterranean, or *Mare Internum* as it was known in Latin. Carthage was a flourishing port city with many ships in its docks, buildings that towered five or six stories, and a wealthy economy, the wealthiest in the world at that time. Everywhere there were roads, large pillars, and statues to Ba'al, god of sky and vegetation. It was a city that glimmered off the sea from the afternoon sun, encompassed by a vast and diverse terrain, ranging from lush grasslands to harsh deserts that tested the perseverance of strong warriors. Within the giant walls of the prosperous city-state was an active market area, filled with merchants, wealthy noblemen, artisans, musicians and peasant stock. Nationals from all over the Mediterranean—Africans, Greeks, Iberians and even Romans—gathered to enjoy the beautiful summer day. There was peace in the region after twenty years of raging war to control the flow of trade in the shared waters. Though Rome had emerged victorious from the war of attrition, both Carthaginians and Romans were weary of battle.

At the center of the metropolis stood the magnificent Suffete. The building's stunning architecture bore strong Greek influences as was evident by the stone pillars, smooth textures, and statues of Ba'al with beard and ram horns symbolizing the strength of the Carthaginian senate. Carthaginian soldiers in full plate mail guarded the stronghold, their long spears poised to confront any unwanted nuisance. Not far from the porcelain governing body dwelled four annoyances of small stature.

Hannibal, a small boy of nine years at the time, peeked over a wall to get a better look at the soldier guarding the stairs leading to the Suffete's balcony. His tall, thin frame allowed him a view that his brothers could not share. He slumped down and reached into his tunic for anything that could be used as a projectile. "We need a distraction." He was met by stares of confusion from his younger siblings, Hanno, Mago and Hasdrubal.

The second oldest, Mago, was eight years too old for his own existence. He carried a mean-spirited look and backed it up with a fiery temper. His short stature only perpetuated his wayward behavior. Much to Hannibal's displeasure, Mago often used Hanno as his favorite wrestling sparring partner.

Hanno, the youngest at six years of age, was chubby, and his tunic never really fit him well. To look into the eyes of Hanno was to gaze into a realm of pure innocence. He was incapable of hurting others, for he did not know how.

Then there was Hasdrubal. He was all brain and little brawn. Even at seven years old, he carried an old spirit. He was the artist, always toting around parchment and colorful stones. As the others contrived a plan of entry, he sketched away, refusing to acknowledge their foolhardiness.

"This is stupid. Father said that we must never come to the Suffete."

"Father said that we must never come to the Suffete." Mago mimicked Hasdrubal and slapped the stone out of his hand in spite. "You are but a little hyena, always fearful."

Hasdrubal picked up the stone and continued to draw, ignoring the repeated teasing by his older brother while Hannibal evaluated the situation. Hannibal's senses were drawn to the stone held by Hasdrubal. "The stone. All we need is for somebody to throw a stone, and we will run to the door." Even at such a young age, Hannibal understood that there was power in numbers.

Mago exposed his maniacal grin. "Hanno should go.

"No. No. No. No." Hanno shook his head emphatically and turned his back, arms folded. His cheeks pouted outward like a blowfish.

"Come on, Hanno," Hannibal pleaded.

"He's too slow, anyway." Mago was always the pessimist.

"Shut up," Hanno screamed, on the verge of crying.

"You shut up!" Mago nudged Hanno in the back of the head.

Hasdrubal drew merrily away in his own world. "This is

foolish."

Hannibal looked to his younger sibling, "Hasdrubal, do you not want to know where father will go?"

"No."

Hannibal curled his lip and adopted more of a trickster persona. He placed a kind hand upon the shoulder of Hanno. "Hanno, you have to go. We are not as quick as you are." Hannibal hated deceiving his little brother, but there were situations in which exploiting his naiveté was justified.

"Really?" Hanno peeked over his shoulder searching for affirmation from the group.

The young Hannibal knew he had him at that point. "Mmm hum. You are a lot faster than Mago, right?"

Mago struggled not to snicker. "Mmm hum."

"They are tricking you, Hanno, like they always do," Hasdrubal said without averting his eyes from his artwork.

Upset, Mago slapped the stone away from Hasdrubal, who stoically picked it up and continued to draw. Mago realized that he needed to remedy the damaging remark. "You are just angry because Hanno is brave, and you are a coward."

Hannibal followed up as a precaution. "Fast and brave."

Hanno smiled and slowly turned around. It did not take much, but he was convinced of his courage and fleetness. The round and brown little boy agreed with the suggestion. "Okay."

Mago snatched the stone from Hasdrubal and handed it to Hanno. Unmoved, Hasdrubal reached into the pouch of his tunic and produced another stone of a different shade. Hasdrubal could see trouble looming from several leagues away. He always could. While Hannibal and Mago watched Hanno from the shadows, Hasdrubal scratched his curly head and began sketching with broad strokes.

Hanno tottered over to a solitary, unsuspecting sentry, a brawny man who could have been easily mistaken for an ebony statue decorated with a black chest plate, helmet, satin tunic and a long spear. Once in throwing distance, Hanno hurled the stone. It struck the soldier's skull with a loud thumping noise that was out of proportion to the damage it actually inflicted. Nonetheless, their gambit worked as planned. The guard was alerted. As soon as he realized that the stone came from the chubby child waving his arms like a bird, he rubbed his bronze helmet in aggravation.

"I'm a bird! I'm a bird!" Hanno flapped away, laughed and ran toward the main entrance in the distance. He really believed he was swift on his feet, and sometimes on the strength of this conviction, he truly was. The soldier gave chase, and they both disappeared into the shadows of the stone hall. "Little bastard!"

Hannibal peeked over the wall again and saw that the sentry was gone. "Okay, let's go." Hannibal and Mago dashed toward the stairs, but Hasdrubal didn't budge.

The two boys made their way up the flight of narrow stairs leading to the balcony that overlooked the council room's floor. They came upon a worn crevice within the wall and huddled near it. One eye at a time, they peaked downward and glimpsed the meeting in progress within the walls of the Suffete. It was a gathering of The Hundred.

In the dimly lit room, twenty robed figures were seated behind an enormous stone podium, all wearing black silk robes with purple trim, the garb of a Carthaginian senator. The lawmakers and judges of the Suffete controlled the destiny of the Carthaginian Empire, with or without the powerless Assembly. Their ages varied, though many were elders. These old warriors snarled at the three men standing below in the shadows of the Suffete Council Room. The men were addressing The Hundred, a body composed of the most powerful and often the wealthiest men in Carthage. Men determined to maintain that status.

Before them on the floor below stood Hamilcar Barca. Tight-jawed and stern, he knew how today's discussion would end. His bronze plate armor glittered from the sunbeams striking through the skylights above, and his black cape hung in thick fashion. With his broad shoulders, bald ebony head and heavy brow, he could intimidate anyone. Nearing the midpoint of his life, much of which had been spent in battle, his tolerance for the Suffete had diminished over the years. After leading the campaign that had crushed a recent mercenary rebellion threatening Carthage, Hamilcar was considered a hero among the common people. Many top officials within the Carthaginian government saw the general as a threat, however. But they were unable to act upon their inner desires. Hamilcar had a sizable army still under his command, ready to spring into action and inflict carnage on any citadel, countryside or sea-faring vessel. Most importantly, Hamilcar had earned the respect of his men during the First Roman War, a loyalty that was not won singularly by the spoils of pillaging.

On his left stood Hasdrubal Bok, a very handsome warrior wearing a silk tunic and black leather armor that blended well with his dark skin. Although he was a young man, his beard gave him an aura of maturity and wisdom. Hamilcar had come to regard this man from Tunis, who had married his daughter Salammbo, as his own son. In return, Hasdrubal Bok pledged his unwavering loyalty to his father-in-law and commander. As Hamilcar's second-in-command, he offered a softer approach to delicate situations—a true politician.

On Hamilcar's right towered Maharbal the Numidian. At over six feet tall, only this young warrior could be so bold as to go bare-chested on the floor of the Suffete. His statuesque body and bald skull bared the scars of countless battles, and he seemed incapable of ever smiling. The African was the best cavalry commander Hamilcar had ever encountered. As Maharbal often explained, "It is in the blood of the Numidians." During the Mercenary War, he was fierce and unforgiving, which was often the reason why he and Hasdrubal Bok clashed on a regular basis. For Hamilcar, it had seem as though a millennium had passed since he first met the child given to him by the swift hand of Ba'al.

Hamilcar separated himself from his two officers and moved closer to the governing body above him. He let his arms rest by his side as his wife Nara had suggested in an effort to subdue his perennial aggressive posture. "The mutiny has been squashed. Therefore, I wish to continue my efforts in Sicily," Hamilcar said. His deep, authoritative intonation silenced the boisterous chamber.

Senator Cobo, a shrewd, little middle-aged man who sat in the center of the towering, dark podium, had never tolerated any form of disobedience in his council. "No. The war is over, General." Cobo had a grating voice that vibrated in one's earlobe, similar to a cat's cry. "Not only did we lose Sicily, but Sardinia, Corsica and Malta have fallen as well."

"Senators, they fell only because I never received the reserve force promised by the Suffete," Hamilcar snapped back.

Murmurs of discontent filled the room. Senator Cobo rolled his eyes to the back of his balding head and rested his bearded and chubby chin upon his hand. "Every man has an excuse, General."

Not long ago, Hamilcar would have lashed out and offered threats in exchange for favors. He had learned over the years that there were moments where diplomacy was key, even with your so-called fellow countrymen. "I make no excuses, Senator, but I cannot win a costly war with the Romans without the support of the Suffete." Hamilcar directed his menacing gaze purposely at the frail African seated in the middle. "No men, no ships . . . it's as though there are some that wish Carthage to fail. Now is the time to take Rome!"

Cobo slammed his palm upon the platform before him. "So speaks our mighty general. We will not accept responsibility for your ineptness! By Ba'al, you even let Regulus reach our homeland!"

Hamilcar gritted his teeth, longing to leap within grasp of Cobo's throat. "That was not my doing!" The time for diplomacy had lost its luster. He had heard this before. These men were corrupt and he knew it. If this were the battlefield, he would watch their heads roll to the amusement of his soldiers. Enough.

But, before he could retaliate, Senator Bragibas, a big, kindly Carthaginian, offered a peaceful solution to their oral melee. He stroked his near-white beard and raised a hand to silence the murmurs of the other senators. "Your loyalty to Carthage will not be forgotten, General Barca, but Carthage has lost. We have already agreed to a tribute for Rome in return for their leniency."

"You trust the Romans?"Hamilcar snorted.

"For now, yes," Bragibas replied.

Hamilcar did trust Bragibas. He had served senator in the

Battle of Ecnomus in the First Roman War. In fact, it was rumored that the young Hamilcar had saved the then captain's life after the Romans had boarded their ship. Of course, the origin of this tale was unknown. Hamilcar raised his index finger and waved it before a word left his lips. "Romans trust only gold and conquest. For Rome, the war is not over!"

"For Carthage, it is. Nevertheless, our dye and metal trading will remain strong." Resigned to the reality of the situation, Bragibas closed his eyes and searched his soul for a solution.

"And like that, we bow down." Hamilcar lowered his head in shame.

"A treaty with tribute, General."

"Yes, I know, Senator. Carthage will pay...in land, gold, ships, slaves, blood." Hamilcar lashed out, "Where does it stop, Senator? Do we wish for our children to inherit our failures?"

"Your failures, General," Cobo interjected, "your failures! This discussion is finished!"

"My children will not be slaves to Rome!" Hamilcar eyed Cobo with a frightening glare.

Senator Bragibas tried, in his ultimate wisdom, to diffuse the situation. "General, your services are needed in Hispania. You are to take with you several quinqueremes, vessels, cavalry and infantry. We must defend Hispania from the Romans as well as from the Gaul and protect our trade routes and mines."

Hamilcar was exasperated with the hand he had been dealt. They were once again turning their backs on a warrior who had dedicated his entire life to the service of his people. "You send a soldier to where there is no battle."

"It is battle, General, that has nearly destroyed Carthage."

Cobo waved the Carthaginian general away. "We are simple merchants. The wages of war are too costly."

Hamilcar moved in closer, to within a few feet below Cobo. The sheer force of his presence made many of the senators lean back in their personal thrones and take heed to what he was going to say.

"What do you know of battle, Senator? I have dedicated my life to Carthage, to defending it from those who would see it fall. And now you wish me to release my bitterness? To forget the blood spilled by my men?"

"We ask for your obedience, General Barca. It is our wish only to save Carthage," Bragibas said.

"Of course, Senator." Hamilcar let out a placating laugh and turned his back on his superiors, an insult of high proportions. With a maniacal smile, he strode toward his two officers, his cape snapping with every move. "But, I shall say this. Rome will not be satisfied with just Sicily. In the end, they want Carthage."

Hamilcar, Hasdrubal Bok and Maharbal began to exit the silent hall until Hamilcar turned back to the council, compelled to finish his thought. "And if that happens, no one will be safe from their slave ships. My riches will not protect me, nor will your silk robes. You may bow down to the snake, Senator, but I will not." On his last word, Hamilcar looked upward toward Hannibal and Mago.

"Ahhhhh!" In a panic, Mago fell backwards and sprinted downstairs. But Hannibal, not afraid, stared into the eyes of his father for but a fleeting moment. He was overcome with a turmoil of emotions that seemed to travel over him like a cold, wet breeze. Hamilcar surveyed the Suffete again and exited the Council Room, his heavy footsteps cutting through the silence.

Senator Cobo leaned forward for a last comment to Hamilcar and sneered at the three departing men. "Commanders come and go, but Carthage is forever, General."

Before exiting, Hamilcar paused for a moment. Not yielding to the fire within, he departed the chamber.

Bragibas face Cobo to offer his perspective on what had just occurred. "He is a powerful man. Men follow him." Cobo's eyes narrowed into slits of rage. His cheeks curled and flinched rapidly in an attempt to mask his longstanding hatred.

"Yes, too powerful."

2.

The sun disappeared into the dark Mediterranean as thunderous waves crashed into the majestic bluff. The four sons of Hamilcar Barca had been frolicking around for most of the day before settling down to dangle their legs from the cliff not far from their home. With the exception of the reticent Hasdrubal, who continued to occupy himself with his artistic pursuits, Mago, Hannibal and Hanno competed in a pebble-tossing contest. Mago appeared to have the upper hand with throws traveling twice as far as the others. The feisty young warrior winked with confidence as he searched for the perfect stone for his next toss.

Hannibal had gazed out to the sea for many years. He would imagine the distant lands where his father was thinking of him as well. *What beauty beyond these waters has kept me apart from my father for so long?* Hannibal yearned for an answer to this question, but until now, his first priority was to guide his younger siblings. Such was the responsibility of all first-born sons of Carthage.

"Father is different."

Hannibal casually tossed another rock. "What do you mean, Hasdrubal?"

Hasdrubal searched his creative mind for an answer but tilted his head in confusion. "I do not know. Different."

"He is strange," Mago uttered under his breath.

"Quiet, Mago!" He was their father and Hannibal would never let them disrespect him in such a manner.

"He is!" Mago said.

"I do not care! Father is not strange."

Hasdrubal lowered his parchment and rested his colored stone on his lap. "Mago's right. He does not speak anymore."

"Father was fighting in a war. He is just tired. That is all."

Hannibal stood and searched for the truth within his own young soul. He knew Hamilcar better than any of them and, at the same time, not at all. The man his mother would tell him wondrous stories about had never surfaced before his eyes.

"Hannibal?" Hanno's soft voice chirped as he scratched his face. He would always scratch his face whenever he was nervous or scared, which was usually a daily occurrence.

"Yes, Hanno?"

"Will father die?"

"Father will not die."

Hanno rested his head in his lap in the way a turtle protects itself from harm. "People die in war. What will we do?"

Hannibal leaned over and rested his hand upon Hanno's shoulder. "I guess I will take care of you if Father dies, but he will live forever."

Hanno popped his head out with a huge grin across his chubby cheeks. "Thank you, brother."

"Let's jump!" Mago leaped to his feet and sprinted to the ledge, sliding to a halt right before the edge. Pebbles trickled down into the water below. He was the risk-taker. Many times, Hannibal swore he did it just to get his goat.

Hasdrubal resumed his sketching and waved off his foolish older brother. "Are you crazy?"

Hannibal pointed with conviction. "Mago get away from there!"

"Hannibal, you're just afraid of water!" Mago swayed

back and forth to simulate his intended leap off the sixty-foot-high cliff. "Why do you always take his side?"

"I'm the oldest, so just don't!"

They squared off with icy stares. The two brothers wondered who would surrender to the other's demand. Mago was tempted to jump anyway, but his attention was drawn over their shoulders.

The other boys turned around and saw their father, Hamilcar, staring at them from a distance, standing as a ghost upon the cultivated plains leading to their home. Behind him were several servants milling about, tending to the land. They were not sure how long he may had been standing there, but the boys could all feel that Hamilcar had observed the foursome for some time, gazing at them with the empty expression to which they had grown accustomed. The boys remained motionless as his silhouette approached, its heavy, dark cloak—which offered protection from the slight zephyr blowing off the sea—shrouded Hamilcar's black tunic as it fluttered in the wind.

"Come inside. Darkness approaches." Hamilcar's strong, booming voice, rarely heard by the boys, commanded instant obedience. Without hesitation, Hamilcar turned and trekked up the hill to the large stone dwelling in the distance as daylight gave way to the darkness of night.

Mago, Hasdrubal and Hanno quickly gathered their assortment of playthings and hurried up the steep hill toward their home. Hannibal took a moment to appreciate the violet glow on the horizon. Hannibal's sense of unease heightened as dark clouds and cool air invaded the coastal community from the north shore—an apt metaphor for his fears.

A storm had begun and the rain beating the wooden

window covers worked its way into a melodic thump. Hannibal slept upon bedding on the floor, tossing and turning within the ethereal realm of ghastly dreams. He awoke in a sweat and trundled out of bed. The moist air increased the perspiration that beaded from his forehead to his chin. Hannibal glanced over at Hasdrubal, who was sound asleep on the bedding beside him. It was the murmur of the mumbled voices outside his room that had awoken him. Hannibal wiped the sweat from his eyes and removed the warm, heavy blanket draped over his shoulders. He made his way out the room and into the dark corridor where he staggered to the source of the voices—his parent's private chambers.

Hannibal peeked in and observed his mother and father talking in their usual manner—Nara not understanding why Hamilcar must leave once again and Hamilcar saying very little in rebuttal. The room was illuminated with several oil lamps and tastefully adorned with silk drapery, vases and sculptures of Phoenician gods and goddesses. Hamilcar toured the room in preparation for slumber, extinguishing each lamp while Nara Barca prepared their bedding. She was a beautiful woman with soft eyes, accentuated by her black, silky hair, which cascaded down her robe, pinned at the back. She had the strength that came from being married to a professional soldier, but the man she had fallen in love with on that distant, fateful afternoon, the man who had rescued her, had changed. Hamilcar had lost his purity. Nara felt the rage of a thousand flames burning in his heart.

Hamilcar paced until he found his place before Nara. "He is ready, Nara."

"Why must he go?" Tears flowed from Nara's eyes, more from anger than sorrow. "He is a child."

"He is the oldest."

Nara's hand found her heart and her fluttering tone amplified the pain within her soul. "He is my son."

Unsure of his immediate response, Hamilcar paused for a moment. "He is a son of Carthage." There was a time when he would had never caused his beloved such heartache, intentionally or not. That was before the carnage.

"My son will not die away from his family, his home. The war is over, Hamilcar."

Hamilcar fell on one knee and caressed Nara's trembling hands. "I will teach him." He gently wiped her wet face, seeing again the beautiful auburn hue of the girl he had married eighteen years ago.

She repelled his touch with a soft push of the hand and held tight to Hamilcar's hand. "You will teach him to hate . . . the hate that consumes you."

Hamilcar looked into her eyes and gritted his teeth to suppress his desire to weep. "Hate is what makes a man whole."

"Hamilcar, no one blames you for what happened in Sicily." Nara rested her palm upon the cheek of her long love.

"Silence!" Hamilcar grew angry at any mention of Sicily, a place that filled him with bitterness. He arose, moving away from Nara, who was well aware that Sicily harbored deep regret for him. He continued extinguishing the few remaining lamps. "I have already decided." He hesitated at the final lamp. "In three moons, Hannibal will go to Hispania with me."

Nara resigned herself to defeat and realized that Hamilcar was unable to hear her plea. "There are times I think my husband died in Sicily."

"Perhaps, in time." Hamilcar extinguished the final lamp,

shrouding the room in darkness.

After hearing the conversation, Hannibal crept back to his bedroom and slid into the bedding on the floor. He stared into the darkness. He was excited, yet afraid, knowing such a day would come. Having just learned that he was soon to leave all that he had known, an empty feeling grew inside him. During his nine years in Ba'al's Kingdom, Hannibal had so desired to see other lands, travel to places he had read in the dusty tomes of his father's library. His dreams were about to be realized. No longer would he see distant lands on faded parchment.

Hannibal turned to his brother, who was snoring away on the hay-filled bedding next to him. "Hasdrubal. Hasdrubal. Are you asleep?"

Hasdrubal didn't budge.

"Hasdrubal!" Hannibal whispered.

"Whaaaaaaat?" Hasdrubal sniffled and licked his lips before awaking from his deep slumber.

Hannibal rested on his elbow. "I'm going to Hispania with father."

Hasdrubal was shocked into consciousness, showing more enthusiasm than normal. "Am I going too?"

"I do not know. Maybe not."

"Why are you going alone?"

Hannibal shifted his head, contemplating the answer. "I do not know." He had always understood the importance of being the eldest son. It had been instilled in him since birth. He could not fathom why his father would not take his mother and brothers to Hispania with him. "Maybe, I am the furthest along in my studies."

"Are you afraid?"

"No." Hannibal smiled and his eyes glistened in the moonlight.

"You're never afraid." Hasdrubal turned over on his back and stared into the darkness as well.

"Sometimes I am afraid." Hannibal looked over to Hasdrubal.

Hasdrubal was surprised. Never had he heard Hannibal speak of fear. "When?"

"In my dreams."

"Dreams cannot harm you, Brother." Hasdrubal yawned. He thought it was a fear of something real, tangible. He turned over to complete his night's rest. "You must be careful, Brother."

"I will be, Brother."

Hannibal leaned back in his bed and enjoyed the silence for most of the night. The prospect of his imminent journey filled him with exhilaration, but he was also afraid of falling into another nightmarish dream. Only when he could no longer resist, he fell into a deep sleep.

3.

Hamilcar's ship was a quinquereme, a monstrous wooden vessel with five banks of oars. As it slice through the Mediterranean tides, the Carthaginian officers dressed in tunics and leather armor paced the decks, shouting orders to the Iberian oarsmen (natives of the land now known as Spain) rowing below. Waves pummeled the hull, oars sliced into the sea and African drummers, setting the rhythm for the rowers, pounded out their hypnotic beats. In the distance, six other ships were massing, preparing to escort Hamilcar's vessel.

Portside, Hannibal observed the African coast from the deck. The sun was setting, and on the bow of the ship stood Hamilcar and Hannibal. Hamilcar was vacant of emotion and silent. Hannibal's view went from the sea to his father. He felt as though he was traveling with a stranger, unfamiliar with the thoughts running through Hamilcar's mind. Hannibal's single thought was that he did not want to disappoint his father, his chance to earn his birthright. Hannibal looked to the sea again, bundling himself in a leopard-skin cloak as a strong sea breeze chilled him.

A day had passed, and Hannibal awoke to the sunlight that filtered into the dirty cabin. Hannibal looked for his father in the cot beside him, but Hamilcar was gone. A table filled with seafaring maps slid back and forth with the ship's motion, reminding Hannibal of the sound a carpenter's saw makes when grating against a tree. As soon as Hannibal sat up, a bird landed on the room's portal. It lingered there for a moment before being frightened away by the screams of the seaman on the bow.

"New Carthage! New Carthage! New Carthage!"

Hannibal made his way up to the deck. In the distance, he saw the beautiful green hills of southern Hispania where several stone buildings and large statues of Ba'al littered the plains. It was just as he had envisioned it. Unlike the outskirts of Carthage, with its spots of dry desert, Hispania was home to lush, green hills and rich, fertile pastures upon which livestock lazily grazed.

A regiment of soldiers greeted the ship as it coasted into the port of New Carthage. Young Hannibal was intrigued by the men's wide spectrum of skin tones, an indication that they had arrived from disparate lands. Even their armor varied from unit to unit. Some were covered in fur while others donned ratty garments. To Hannibal, the paler warriors seemed very tall, and he wondered why their bodies were adorned with so few coverings.

The ramp of the ship lowered, and Hamilcar, Hannibal and the other seaman disembarked onto the extended dock. Hannibal, who was struggling to carry his medium-size sack, trailed behind his father. Hamilcar's first officer and son-in-law Hasdrubal Bok and several soldiers were assembled to greet them. They were joined by two others, including a man named Gisgo.

Clad in leather armor that fitted him like a glove, this honorable young African from Tunisia had a slender build and a pristine appearance. His hairless face caught Hannibal by surprise; he had never seen a clean-shaven warrior before. Gisgo had enlisted in Hamilcar's army during the Mercenary War, and much like the other officers, he revered Hamilcar as a leader. Gisgo wasn't a brilliant officer, but he was an excellent tactician whose loyalty to Carthage was without question. He immediately gave Hamilcar the salutation of fist to chest.

The other man, named Synhus, was a fragile, small, bald and middle-aged African. His face was leathery and adorned with multiple piercings. The robe he wore gave him an air of wisdom and spirituality. But his eyes frightened Hannibal. They were far too big for his face; so wide that they never appeared to blink.

Hasdrubal Bok placed his hand upon his heart. "Welcome, Father. I prayed to Ba'al for your safe travel."

Hamilcar comforted Hasdrubal Bok with a hand on his shoulder. "It was very safe. However, I am tired. See to your brother and brief me in my command chamber at light's end." Hamilcar continued on, followed by his bodyguards and Synhus.

Momentarily fazed by Hamilcar's coldness, Hasdrubal Bok reached down and placed a hand on Hannibal's shoulder. "Well, Brother, welcome to Hispania. I am sorry I did not see you while I was in Carthage. Father insisted I come to Hispania at once."

"I am grateful for your kind thoughts," Hannibal said while lowering his head to further express his gratitude.

"Anyway, it's good to see you." Hasdrubal Bok smiled. "Your sister eagerly awaits your arrival before she sails for Tunis. This is Gisgo, my second in command."

"Ah!" Gisgo placed his hand upon Hannibal's shoulder. "So, you are Hannibal. You are very tall for your age. You will make a fine soldier someday."

Hasdrubal Bok stooped to one knee. "You are hungry, I suppose?"

"Yes, Brother." Hannibal nodded.

"Well, it is good for you that we have enlisted the best cooks in the Mediterranean." Hasdrubal Bok chortled, bringing a smile to Hannibal's young face.

Hasdrubal Bok waved his hand and quickly an Iberian servant scampered up to take Hannibal's sack. Hannibal, confused by the gesture, snatched it back and held on tight. They tugged back and forth until Hannibal yanked the sack with conviction, freeing the man's grasp. Hasdrubal Bok intervened, handing the sack to the servant, who lowered his head and stepped back.

Hasdrubal Bok was amused by Hannibal's naïveté. "It is fine. You have much to learn."

Warriors that are servants as well? Hannibal thought.

Together, they took the horse-drawn wagon to Hamilcar's stronghold.

4.

Hamilcar, Hasdrubal Bok, Maharbal, Gisgo and several lieutenants sat around a long porcelain table, studying a large map of Hispania. The map was covered with miniature figures that represent machines of war—siege engines, battering rams and such. Torches were posted throughout the room, bathing it in adequate light. The walls were adorned with statuettes depicting warriors in various poses. This was Hamilcar's battle chamber, located within the brick walls of his fortress in New Carthage.

"And what of the Illergetes?" Hamilcar stroked his beard, focused on the archaic map below him.

"Many have fled just north of the Pyrenees," Gisgo responded.

Hamilcar's frustration soon revealed itself to the men he had appointed as his military staff. "The mines are important to the Suffete. We must push the Celtiberians out of the west. Why is it taking this long?"

"We have many allies among the tribes. We can control the mines with little bloodshed," Hasdrubal Bok volunteered.

"We need no allies," Maharbal snarled. His biceps flexed as he tightened his fist. Maharbal despised political resolution, preferring to settle his disputes in the course of battle. "My cavalry on horseback will be enough."

"I grow weary of these excuses," Hamilcar said in his deep, bellowing voice.

"The men are dying from boredom, General. We need a battle to be reborn," Maharbal pleaded.

"The men are content, Father. Maharbal speaks for his cavalry only." Hasdrubal Bok took offense at the remark, regarding it as a direct attack on his command.

"Unlike you, Captain, Numidians do not fear battles," Maharbal said with a maniacal grin.

Hasdrubal Bok pounded the ivory table and sought refuge from his father-in-law. "I am his commander, yet he continues to let his mouth move with disobedience!"

"Silence!" Hamilcar was infuriated with Hasdrubal Bok. He demanded more from his officers, especially those who carried the Barca name, irregardless of the bloodline. "That is the price of leadership. Have you not learned anything that I have taught you?"

Hasdrubal Bok raised his hand in resolve. "Yes, Father. But there is always a leader, and others must follow."

"I will not follow a politician." Maharbal enjoyed stirring Hasdrubal Bok at every opportunity.

Hasdrubal Bok moved to within inches of Maharbal. "You are a fool!" The saliva from his clenched teeth splattered into the air and upon the chest of Maharbal.

"Enough!" Hamilcar said with a tight jaw. "How dare you bicker before me!"

As a rule, both Hasdrubal Bok and Maharbal were respectful of their father-and-son relationship with Hamilcar, but there were times when Hamilcar's words would scar them deeper than any blade. They dropped their heads to avoid the sharp, reproachful gaze of the Carthaginian general. Content with their remorseful response, Hamilcar pointed to an area on the map as the officers moved in closer. "We must replenish our supplies before winter. Gisgo, enlist a few of our Celtiberians as scouts to various tribes. Have them offer their chieftains an alliance."

Gisgo nodded in agreement. "And what of the tribes that resist, General?"

"We shall push them into the sea."

A smile filled Maharbal's face, but the others were frozen. Never had Hamilcar appeared so rash, enraged and merciless. In recent campaigns to subjugate the rebellious mercenary army, Hasdrubal Bok had watched his stepfather transform into a man bent on immediate results and squashing all those who dared to challenge him. An unstable volcano had begun its cycle, and only Hasdrubal Bok wondered when it would run its course and reach its death throes.

"I will issue your orders, Father," Hasdrubal Bok said as Hamilcar walked toward the entrance of the chamber.

Hamilcar paused without turning about. "Both of you were correct. But those who choose not to fight together will surely perish together." Hamilcar departed with two Carthaginian guards following behind.

Hasdrubal Bok stared at the map as the others left the room.

Not far from the adjourning military strategy meeting, the young Hannibal looked off into the darkness from the roof of the tallest spire within Hamilcar's encampment. In the distance, Hannibal could see over the massive walls that protected his father's fortress. His eyes followed a line of Numidian horsemen with torches that were riding off toward the coast. Hannibal assumed that the muscular cavalry was destined for the warships silhouetted on the port of New Carthage.

"War never sleeps." It was then that the fragile-looking African with bright, frightening eyes startled Hannibal. Synhus's long, heavy robe gave him the impression of gliding instead of walking as he passed a shivering Hannibal. Synhus bore a curious smirk that, in Hannibal's colorful imagination, only added to his air of mystery. "I often come here to see what the stars may foretell. It can be a dangerous place for a boy."

"I'm sorry."

Synhus put his index finger to his lips and grinned. As Synhus gazed into the horizon, Hannibal stayed put, afraid to go near the spiritual figure.

"It is remarkable, is it not?" Synhus spoke to the boy without diverting his eyesight from the stars.

"Remarkable?" Hannibal said to Synhus's back, careful not to move any closer to the mystical figure.

"How we never enjoy all that Ba'al has to offer us. Your father has never been able to appreciate these gifts. Ba'al is beyond war. He is of truth."

"I do not understand."

Synhus sat on the stone roof beneath him with his legs crossed, still with his back to Hannibal. "I am Synhus. What do you enjoy in life, Young Hannibal?"

Hannibal was perplexed for a moment. "I like to learn of places far away."

"Far away places?" This intrigued Synhus.

"I want to know about the places my father has traveled."

"Learned in Greek, are you?"

"No," Hannibal said in shame.

"You will have to learn. The greatest writings are from Greece. I will teach you."

A cold breeze passed and Hannibal adjusted his tunic for warmth. It felt unnatural to him.

"You are afraid of me. I remind you of one of your many nightmares," Synhus whispered.

"I don't have nightmares, and I'm not afraid." It never occurred to Hannibal that the man before him knew his innermost secrets. Synhus practiced the unseen, the elements both feared and respected by men.

"It is nothing to be ashamed of. I, too, was once afraid. Many believe the emotion is centered in the mind. Where it truly comes from is the heart. You are afraid, but you do not know why."

"I do not understand." Hannibal moved closer, feeling braver than a few moments ago. "You speak strangely."

Synhus let out a bellowing laugh. "Do I? Perhaps."

Hannibal maneuvered to get a forward glimpse of Synhus, but maintaining a safe distance. He was now drawn in.

"Will I see other lands?"

"You will. I can see that your destiny lies in another land."

Soon, Hannibal was able to see the face of Synhus. His eyes were closed and his lips were shut tightly.

"It is dark and foreboding." Synhus's words hung heavily in the chilly air.

At that moment, Hannibal became horrified and realized that during their entire conversation, Synhus had never used his mouth. "Magic!" Hannibal stumbled, jolted by what he had witnessed. He scurried to the corner of the roof and curled up for protection.

Synhus faced Hannibal. "It is the voice of Ba'al Ammon. He simply speaks through me."

Hannibal uncovered his face. "Speaks through you?"

"A young man must rest. Sleep, Young Hannibal."

His final three words overpowered Hannibal's soul, compelling him to shut his eyes. As another zephyr passed,

Hannibal laid motionless, succumbing to a powerful wave of deep slumber.

Hannibal's hands were bloodstained. A lion sat some thirty feet away, studying the nine-year-old young man, who was now his prey. Hannibal's eyes widened as the lion rose to all fours. He rubbed his hands to see if the blood would come off. It did not; he only managed to smear it into a deeper, thicker paste. When he looked down at his feet, he noticed four small lion cubs lying dead in a pool of blood. The echo of the lion's roar startled Hannibal, causing him to tremble. The animal lunged at him at full pace, poised for the kill. In his desperation, Hannibal twisted around to flee, but he soon found that he was on the edge of a cliff. Some one hundred feet below was a thick fog that hid the base of the precipice. Hannibal shot one final glance at the lion before turning to face the cliff.

Hannibal awoke screaming and leaped off the furry bedding. His heart was pounding and his eyes darted left and right in search of the lion. They found a dusty lab only that was littered with tomes decorated with symbols, skeletal remains of strange creatures and several decanters filled with liquids of various colors. Plants of different species hung from the ceiling, giving the large space the appearance of a small jungle.

Hannibal could hear the faint sounds of a little girl singing in a language that he could not decipher. Pushing his way through the flora and skeletal fauna, he followed the innocent melody and discovered its source. A boyish looking Greek girl, no more than five, hummed as she plucked the leaves from a plant. She was dressed in a tunic, and her protruding legs swung off the edge of a large chair. She instantly froze at the sight of Hannibal and ceased her singing.

"What are you singing?"

The girl jumped off the chair and ran past Hannibal out the room.

"Wait!" Hannibal tried to block her escape, but she slipped through his grasp. Before Hannibal could give chase, he turned to face Synhus. "I do not understand."

"Imilce is such a reticent child," Synhus said while shaking his head in remembrance. "For a child to see her parents die at such a young age is a travesty."

"Was that Greek?"

"At your father's request, I will teach you many languages. The songs will be my addition. Today your lessons begin. We shall start with Plutarch." Synhus searched methodically through several texts on the shelves, his index finger tapping each one. "Here we are." He selected a huge tome from the shelf and plopped the book on the table in front of Hannibal. Dust flew into Hannibal's eyes. As Hannibal opened the book, Synhus unexpectedly placed another book on top. "And volume two, of course." Hannibal's jaw dropped as the healer set a third volume down. Synhus rejoiced at one book in particular. "Ah, Life of Timoleon. My personal favorite."

"I do not read Greek." The length of the stacked books exceeded Hannibal's height.

Synhus paused for a second in contemplation. "You are very correct. Those three will have to do for today."

Before Hannibal could protest, Synhus slapped the top of the stack of books, which kicked up dust directly into Hannibal's face. "Aaaaaaachuu!"

5.

A dusty field under the burning sun served as a target practice arena for young soldiers in training. Several Carthaginian officers lined the side of the narrow path leading to a large wooden target. Hamilcar and Hasdrubal Bok looked on as a young Carthaginian officer sent a javelin whirling fifty feet through the air until it connected squarely in the middle. The officer bowed to the approving grunts of the onlookers.

It was now Hannibal's turn. The boy approached the rack of javelins and selected one that was almost twice his height. He gave his father a final look and sprinted to the line. On his last footstep, Hannibal launched the spear at the target. It fell short. Catching his breath, the young Hannibal was able to glimpse the disappointed expression of his father.

Hamilcar folded his arms and sighed to shield his embarrassment. There was an eerie silence among the officers. "Another," Hamilcar shouted in a deep, commanding voice.

Hannibal scrambled over to the polearm stand and selected another javelin. He sprinted and hurled the second spear at the target. For a moment, it appeared as though it was going to connect, but it sailed pitifully over the target.

Hasdrubal Bok could remember his training as a young warrior. He understood the difficulty of the tests, which had to be performed one after another. Failures were to be expected, of course, but the expectations were overwhelming, particularly for a soldier who carried the Barca name. He knew what that meant and he could empathize with the young Hannibal.

Hasdrubal Bok turned to Hamilcar. "Perhaps the length."

"Do not make excuses for your inadequacies. Are you training him or not?" Hamilcar hissed.

Exasperated, Hamilcar approached Hannibal and, without hesitation, slapped his son to the ground. The startled youth looked at his father with eyes wide open. He was afraid, terrified that the towering man had forgotten that the boy who cowered before him was his son.

"You are shaming our family name! Arise!"

Hannibal did not cry as most children would have done at his age. He pushed himself up with the fear of Ba'al showing in his face.

"Another," Hamilcar said through clenched teeth.

Hannibal selected another javelin. A single tear trickled down his face. He brushed it away and dried his hand on the cloth of his tunic. With determination he sprinted past Hamilcar and launched the spear at the target.

It missed.

Hannibal's head fell to his chest, and deep feelings of failure filled his heart. "I'm sorry, Father."

Furious, Hamilcar grabbed a bundle of spears and slammed them down at Hannibal's feet. He gave Hannibal one final glare and departed, trailed by the other officers. Hannibal remained there alone on the field in sorrow.

The day soon became night, and Hannibal remained on the training ground. Hannibal's light tunic soon draped lazily on his shivering frame due to the merciless rainfall. He was exhausted, hungry and wet. He continued to throw javelins at the target. The many spears that went astray covered the ground around the thick wooden box. In disgust, he selected the last javelin, wiped the rain from his eyes and studied the target during a lengthy pause. You are shaming our family name, he recalled Hamilcar's words, echoing in his thoughts. Anger had filled his heart as he dashed through the mud and hurled the javelin with all his might. It whistled through the air until Hannibal heard the silver point splinter the wood. It was embedded in the target. It had connected. For just a moment, Hannibal gawked at the fractured wood, his chest heaving up and down. However, instead of celebrating, he cried. Indeed, Hannibal wept on that field for most of the night, wiping the mud across his face. He was in an unknown environment with unfamiliar individuals, including his father. He was lost, sorely longing for the safety of his brothers.

In the shadows, Hamilcar observed his son from the heights of the wall surrounding the field and allowed himself to smile. He stood there and watched Hannibal cry for home, for Carthage. Within, it tore at the general's heart. Hamilcar feared that his first son's sole memories of his father would be dark ones, but he knew that he must follow Ba'al's will for retribution. He would have to ask for forgiveness when all was done.

6.

Bithynia, Asia Minor—182 B.C.

The aged Hannibal took another sip of wine and winced once more from the gash in his abdomen as Scipio looked on. The rain outside the inn was heavier.

Scipio the Younger stood, exasperated by the long time he had spent sitting down. His armor clinked against the wooden chair. "I see a man who could not let things end as they should."

"Rome slowly ate away at his soul," Hannibal agreed.

"And you followed his path." Peering out of the window at the cobblestone street below, Scipio noticed several legionnaires from his century. They remained at attention, still awaiting his orders. The centurion looked up to receive a reassuring wave from Scipio.

Hannibal twirled the hairs of his beard with his finger and thumb and considered what Scipio had said. In his heart, he knew at that moment that the Roman was correct. But as a child, how could he have ever known? Wasn't it natural for a son to crave the love of his father? No. He could never blame his father for the path he had taken.

"Duty," Hannibal said. "After ten years...ten years of battling unwelcoming natives, memories of Carthage soon faded. Everything I know today, I learned in Hispania."

Central Spain—228 B.C.

Hamilcar's encampment was situated near a sparkling tributary that flowed north of the Tagus River. The base was littered with many tents, housing for the soldiers who were now busily preparing for the night, anxious to complete their tasks and enjoy repast before the sun disappeared beyond the horizon. Drumbeats could be heard throughout the grassy hills of Hispania. This had been their home away from New Carthage for many years, throughout their campaign to subjugate the Celtiberi tribes.

Several Carthaginian, Numidian, and Iberian officers had separated from the foot soldiers and gathered to form a small, circular human arena. The men were fixated on Hannibal and Hasdrubal Bok, who were armed with wooden staffs and facing each other in a heated practice match inside the circle. Hannibal had matured into a strong, tall, slender and confident nineteen-year-old man. He shaved his head as many Carthaginian men did upon reaching manhood. Although Hannibal was still unable to grow the full beard that he desired, he was very proud of his goatee, which was many years in coming. At the moment, the bristles around his mouth were crimson as a small trickle of blood leaked from both his mouth and that of Hasdrubal Bok, who was ten years older and craftier. Hasdrubal Bok twirled his staff with extreme confidence as the two circled each other. Both men had removed their breastplates for more dexterity, which left their tunics exposed to the elements and covered in dirt.

"Of all the writings you have read, Brother, should you not have read one on combat? I do feel responsible since I have trained you the most," Hasdrubal Bok lamented.

"You have trained me on what it means to have a huge

mouth," Hannibal replied.

Hannibal brought his staff overhead and lunged toward Hasdrubal Bok with a whirling motion. Instinctively, Hasdrubal Bok ducked to one knee as the weapon whizzed inches from his pate. As retribution, he raised one end of his staff up and struck Hannibal's chin, launching Hannibal into the air and then flat on his back. A splash of blood expectorated from Hannibal's mouth. The pain stung more as the rowdy crowd cheered while Hasdrubal Bok stood over the fallen Hannibal. He endured the occasional banter from the onlookers.

"Are you okay, Brother?" Hasdrubal Bok chuckled.

Hannibal searched his lungs in desperation for air.

"Training has ended for today." Hasdrubal Bok offered Hannibal a hand up, but Hannibal waved his gesture off and regained his feet.

"Ended?" Hannibal raised one eyebrow.

Hasdrubal Bok waved his younger sibling off and began to walk away. Not willing to concede, Hannibal picked up a small rock and hurled it at the back of Hasdrubal Bok's head.

Thonk.

Hasdrubal Bok was incensed. He tramped back toward Hannibal. "That is your biggest weakness. You never know when to accept defeat. Now I'm going to--"

Before his brother-in-law could finish his threat, Hannibal launched his staff like a javelin. Without time to react, the staff bounced right off Hasdrubal Bok's forehead, causing the Tunisian commander to fall onto his back. Hannibal sauntered over and looked down at Hasdrubal Bok.

"I do know that when a man loses control of his emotions, even the obvious becomes invisible to him."

Hasdrubal Bok moaned as he touched the fresh bruise.

"Such trickery is useless in battle."

"It wasn't much of a trick. Hannibal extended a hand of support. "Are you okay, Brother?"

Later that night in Hamilcar's command tent, Hamilcar gathered his officers to discuss and celebrate their victories. He seemed more content than usual. Although the silver mines were now beginning to take root and Hispania would soon fall under complete Carthaginian rule, Hamilcar was never a demon of conquest. Everyone knew of his desire to regain Sicily and destroy the Roman citadel, neither being accomplished, nor planned, for that matter. Hamilcar was under the scrutiny of the Suffete, which maintained a tight rein on their most successful military leader. The governing body had become paranoid, alarmed by the treachery of past commanders, who, driven by their thirst for power, had attempted to overthrow the Suffete. Most of the spoils Hamilcar's mercenary army acquired were shipped to the treasury of Carthage.

Though much more spacious than the common soldiers' mobile dwellings, Hamilcar's inconspicuous tent had no furniture, except for the straw pillows that he, Hannibal, Hasdrubal Bok, Maharbal, Synhus, two Carthaginian junior officers and one Iberian officer were seated upon. Together, they raised their wine-filled goblets in a toast.

Hasdrubal Bok hoisted his drink once more. "The Celtiberians are in order now, General. Again, we have won."

"Yes, but many remain alive. We should have taken their blood," Maharbal said. The Numidian was the only one without wine. He saw inebriation as a barbaric way to escape one's fears. Maharbal rejoiced in the finality of death. It was one truth that no man could alter to his gain.

Hamilcar chortled for a moment. He and Maharbal had

faced many a battle together. "We must kill only when it means victory, Maharbal." Although Hamilcar disagreed with the brutal tactics that Maharbal utilized with his cavalry, Hamilcar understood the necessity of having an officer with the capacity for ruthlessness.

There was agreement among the men. However, Hannibal needed more clarification. "Always, Father?" The laughter ceased and the men were silent, waiting for a response from their general.

"It is true, part of me enjoys the glory of combat." Hamilcar, impressed with Hannibal's having the fortitude to question him, shared a smile with his son. "However, as a leader, one must consider the end result before one sacrifices one's men."

"Father speaks of politics. A man's head can be sharper than the blade," Hasdrubal Bok added.

Hannibal remained confused. These were not words he had ever heard from his father or brother-in-law. They were never part of his teachings. He had to voice his discontent. "But there are those who wish for war. You've told me of Rome, Father, the treaties they have broken, and the deception they have revealed. Who would be allies with such a people?"

"Politics as a weapon my son, not as a joining of brotherhood. You see, understanding the politics of a people is just as useful to a commander as knowing the strength of his army."

Hannibal's eyes widened with discovery. The young warrior held the hilt of his short sword tightly. "I see. Whatever it takes to motivate the people to your end result. Use it against them, their selfishness, their doubt--"

"And their fear," Hamilcar said.

Maharbal was offered a drink by the Carthaginian officer seated beside him. Maharbal's overbearing presence dispelled the man's foolish notion. "The alliances with these savage natives will never last. We should have destroyed them all, especially the tribes that refused to fight." Maharbal took the cup and slammed it on the floor before him. "Weak! They make my stomach twist."

"It takes more than destruction to control the hearts of men," Synhus opined. He flashed his usual grin as his eyes focused on Maharbal.

"The last prophecies of a dying man." Maharbal bursted into laughter. "Hamilcar may believe in your witchery, but I do not."

"Are you always so untrusting?" Hasdrubal Bok said.

"No. only when I am awake," Maharbal responded with a snarl.

As they all laughed, Hamilcar stood.

"Father, where are you going?" Hannibal said.

"It is time for me to rest." Hamilcar took a deep breath. "I will leave at dawn."

Hasdrubal Bok stumbled to his feet with determination. "I shall accompany you."

Hamilcar stopped short of the silk cloth-covered exit. "No, you must bring the main army back to New Carthage. I will take my guards and see you there."

Hamilcar departed and Hannibal dashed behind his father. Two Carthaginian soldiers stood guard just outside the tent that sat atop a hill overlooking the dark green valley. In the distance, the campfires of the soldiers below appeared as fireflies in the night.

"Father?"

Hamilcar turned. "Something is wrong, I know."

"I will ride with you in the morning."

Hamilcar smiled and placed his hands upon Hannibal's shoulders. "You have become all that I knew you would. The next step must be taken."

Hannibal was overwhelmed by the remark. He had not heard the approval of his father for a long time. Tears filled his eyes. "You cannot..."

Hamilcar surveyed the wide-open plains of the Carpetani, a native clan of Hispania. "I have always enjoyed riding my steed across these lands." Hamilcar took solace in their simplicity.

Hannibal disagreed. This was the first time that his father would not be there for him. Since their journey to Hispania ten years ago, Hamilcar had maintained a watchful eye over every aspect of Hannibal's growth—his teachings, his training, his rite of passage. Hannibal felt alone once again. He had the heart of a warrior but the heart of a lost boy as well.

"When you come to New Carthage, we will ride together. I have so much I wish to tell you," Hamilcar said, hoping to reassure his son. Hamilcar released Hannibal. He took a step back and gave him a stern look.

Hannibal regained his inner strength and posture. "I would like that, Father."

Hamilcar grasped Hannibal by the collar of his tunic and offered him more words of insight. "These men are no more than mercenaries." Hamilcar pulled Hannibal closer. "They fight for riches and lust for women to be taken. But they do not follow me simply out of thirst for the treasure that fills their coffers after each campaign. That is why they do not rebel or choose to flee into the night. They follow me because every man searches for someone to follow, someone he can trust. If you are not always a symbol of strength, they will not trust you."

Hamilcar released his son, who nodded in comprehension. Thereupon, Hamilcar left Hannibal standing alone, deciphering what his father had said.

"I will see you in Carthage, Father."

"Yes." Without facing Hannibal, the teary-eyed Hamilcar walked away.

7.

The smoke from the extinguished breakfast fires streamed into the sunny horizon as Iberian, Carthaginian, Numidian, Libyan, Algerian and Balearic soldiers prepared for their march to New Carthage. Tents were dropped and horses and oxen were being fitted for hauling. In the distance, Hannibal rode his horse at a rapid gallop out of the camp. The glare from his helmet caught the eyes of Hasdrubal Bok and Maharbal, who were standing by the command tent.

"He wants to ride with Hamilcar and the general is at least a half a night's ride away," Maharbal said.

Hasdrubal Bok adjusted the strings on his leather bracers and took a deep breath. "What a young fool! Send some of your horsemen to ensure that he makes it there in one piece."

The Edetani region gave way to lush hills of green, dotted with sunflowers. Ten leather-clad Carthaginian soldiers made their way through the meadow on horseback. Hamilcar, who had assumed the fourth spot in the caravan, blocked the glare of the sun with his free hand. As they moved up a steep incline, Hamilcar's horse became startled. The clamor of hooves and the animal's fearful snorts nearly threw Hamilcar from his saddle. Soon the other steeds became excited. Seconds later he managed to regain control of his mount, and the horses settled down. However, he still felt uneasy. He scanned the hills, his eyes darting from side to side beneath his heavy brow. Something was wrong.

"Men, stand ready!"

The whistles of short javelins zipped past Hamilcar, some piercing the bodies of his escort. Three soldiers fell to the ground immediately. Hamilcar and the remaining six dismounted with haste and searched for cover behind their horses. The javelins continued to whistle overhead.

"Take cover, General!" shouted a soldier just before a javelin impaled him through the upper chest, splashing blood on Hamilcar's face.

Over the hill and out of the sun raced thirty bearded barbarians dressed in animal skins and brandishing swords. Their howls of aggression were aimed at the Carthaginian party.

"Celtiberians?" Hamilcar unsheathed his sword and readied the blade.

The Celtiberians rushed in with disheveled auburn hair flying and iron long swords flailing away. The remaining five Carthaginian soldiers fanned out to meet the marauders. They fought fiercely but succumbed to the overwhelming numbers, taking only a few of the Celtiberians to the grave with them.

Hamilcar stood alone, sword extended. He pivoted, looking for an advantage over the circling party of Celtiberians. "Which cave dweller wishes to taste my blade first? Perhaps you?"

Hamilcar slashed the man closest to him across his throat before the warrior could raise his sword in defense. The man fell as his blood sprayed in the air. Another Celtiberian lurched forward with a jab of his sword. Hamilcar deflected the attempt with his sword, spun around, and impaled the unbalanced man in the back. The Celtiberian screamed in pain and crumbled to the ground.

The Celtiberians grew timid before Hamilcar. Each was looking for an opening to attack—circling, stalking. Another

Celtiberian leaped into melee with Hamilcar. Their swords locked, and they fought for control—pushing and pulling until a kick in the abdomen from Hamilcar brought the soldier to his knees. With a battle cry, Hamilcar raised his sword to split the man's head like ripe melon.

Whiz. Thump.

The javelin caught Hamilcar in the abdomen. He screeched in agony and turned around to see who had launched the deadly projectile. "Aralas!" Hamilcar's eyes widened.

Near the top of the hill sat a man on horseback, draped in animal fur as well. The man removed the wolf's skull from atop his head, revealing a pudgy face and, appropriately enough, the shifty eyes of a wolf. His long, gray hair flowed with the wind.

Hamilcar dropped to his knees and coughed up blood. He attempted to remove the javelin from his midsection with no success. The world around him became blurry. He wavered in a haze.

Aralas, still on his horse, approached Hamilcar as the surrounding Celtiberians divided to let him through. Hamilcar endeavored to stand but rolled on his back, too weak from the heavy loss of blood. With a maniacal smirk, Aralas looked down on the pitiful Hamilcar. "You should have retired by now, perhaps, General?"

Hamilcar gritted his blood-covered teeth. "Scipio's pet. Where is your master? Afraid to do his cowardly deeds himself?"

Aralas reached down to yank the javelin from Hamilcar's wound. Grunting with resistance, Hamilcar held on to his end, until the javelin tore away from his body. Flesh dangled from the spear's tip. "You Roman bastard, you will die! All of you bastards will die!"

"Not in your lifetime, General." Aralas relaunched his javelin into Hamilcar's chest, piercing his leather armor between the bronze chest plates of his corselet.

Hamilcar took one last breath and died.

"That is one." Aralas yanked the spear away and rode off.

When Hannibal arrived atop the hill, the sun had begun its fateful decline. He discovered bodies strewn about the meadow and galloped past the slain Celtiberians slowly with his sword extended, poking to see if there were any hints of life. Hannibal brought his horse to a halt, eyes darting from side to side in search of his father. He was forced to dismount once he saw Hamilcar lying motionless in the field. Hannibal raced to the side of Hamilcar and fell to his knees. He struggled to lift the limp body into his lap. Eventually, he was able to caress his father's upper body and rest his head in his arms. He gazed at his father one last time and closed Hamilcar's eyes with a brush of his fingers.

"Together again. You said we would ride together." A single tear trickled down his cheek. "There is truth in dreams. I should not have let you go. I should not have let you go."

Hannibal collapsed upon his father's bloodstained chest, and his cries echoed over the hills.

8.

The dark waters of the Mediterranean blended with the night sky, and the bright half moon welcomed the event that was about to take place. The torchlights of thousands of soldiers in formation created a somber seacoast landscape. On a floating skiff lay the body of Hamilcar, which was dressed only in a loincloth. Painted symbols and runes telling of past deeds covered his entire body; tightly bound timber and straw lay beneath him. In a steady hypnotic beat, a massive Numidian soldier pounded on a huge drum.

Synhus, his face painted with stark white paste, began chanting in the ancient Phoenician language, simultaneously rubbing oil over Hamilcar. He stepped away from the body with hands extended. He reached for a lit torch that was stationed near the body and clutched it.

The drumbeats ceased playing.

Synhus approached Hannibal, Hasdrubal Bok, Maharbal and Gisgo. Each man bore a look of great sadness, except for Maharbal, whose eyes were even sharper than his snarl. Synhus placed the torch into Hannibal's hands and stepped out of his path as the young man made his way toward Hamilcar.

Hannibal gazed at the face of his father, but the tears could no longer fall. There is a moment after death when those left behind must conquer sorrow and not become consumed with thoughts of regret. Hannibal refused to cry for his father anymore. He remembered what Hamilcar told him the last time they would ever speak to each other. Men follow strength, and Hannibal would not disappoint his father by shedding a tear. Hannibal slowly lit the timber below Hamilcar's body and watched as the flames engulfed it. He pushed the skiff away.

Hamilcar floated off into the Mediterranean from whence he was born.

Later that night, Hasdrubal Bok, Hannibal, Maharbal, Gisgo and Synhus gathered within the conference chamber to discuss the aftermath of Hamilcar's death. They were still dressed in their ceremonial armor. The torches created mysterious shadows on the walls.

Maharbal sprang from his seat. "Why do we wait!? You know the Romans killed him, Hasdrubal!"

"Would you take such a tone with Hamilcar, Maharbal? I am in command now, and you will obey me," Hasdrubal Bok replied with a soft intonation.

Maharbal circled the wooden table and leaned down to within inches of Hasdrubal Bok's contorted face. Hasdrubal Bok stood to bring their piercing glares on equal standings.

"I will obey my general. Even when you are weak I will obey," Maharbal said.

"Perhaps I should free you from your bondage as cavalry commander?" Hasdrubal Bok said, his neck throbbing with rage.

"Perhaps I should free you from your bondage as general?"

Hasdrubal Bok unsheathed his short sword, but Maharbal did not flinch. Indeed, his grin only tempted Hasdrubal Bok to strike. Maharbal had waited for this moment for years. Fortunately, Gisgo stepped in and prevented a melee from breaking out between the two men.

"General! Commander!" Always the rational one, Gisgo owed his life to Hamilcar and would not allow them to disgrace his journey to Ba'al's kingdom.

Synhus poured himself another drink and smirked. "Romans may never get their chance. We may kill ourselves first."

Hannibal looked bewildered. "Maharbal, why do you speak of Romans?"

"You have not told him?" Maharbal chuckled.

"Told me of what, Hasdrubal?"

Hasdrubal Bok returned his sword back to its scabbard, walked over to another table and grabbed a woolly sack. He opened the sack, revealing a Roman short sword. He handed the weapon to Hannibal, who studied it carefully.

"A *gladius*. A weapon carried by a Roman legionnaire. We found it impaled in one of Hamilcar's guards," Hasdrubal Bok said.

"Only forged by the Romans!" Maharbal added.

"What of the Celtiberians who attacked, Father?"

"Most of them escaped the attack, Hannibal. I've sent trackers," Gisgo said.

"The Celtiberians were supplied by the Romans." Hannibal lifted the *gladius* to eye level, and his stare followed the bloodstains that dotted its tip.

Maharbal whispered in Hannibal's ear. "They killed Hamilcar, Hannibal."

"I will not fight another war with the Romans! I will not see Carthage burned to the ground! We have peace." Hasdrubal Bok was defiant.

"Peace. This pseudo-peace is starving Carthage and enslaving Africans!" roared Maharbal. "We've fought many battles together. I too am weary. But it is now that the Romans are at their weakest."

Gisgo interceded. "It is true, my General! The Romans have not fully recovered from our first war. Our navy is much stronger."

For a moment, Hasdrubal Bok contemplated what his officers were saying. And during that moment, he felt the weight that Hamilcar must have had to endure for so long. Now it was his turn to command, and he knew in his soul that Carthage could not withstand another war with Rome. "The Suffete would never approve of it. We will concentrate on Hispania."

Hannibal stood and made his way for the balcony as the men continued to debate retribution and the honor of the Suffete. The stone balcony overlooked the murky Mediterranean Sea, which was glittering from the moon's mystical glow. In the distance, he could see the silhouettes of several tetraremes, ships with four banks of oars. Eventually, the sound of the ocean waves drowned out the argument inside. His thoughts were only of his father. He felt cheated. Hannibal believed that once he made his father proud to call him son, once he became the man that Hamilcar demanded of his first son, they would speak to one another as father and son. Hannibal felt cold and empty, unsure of where his emotions would take him. The pain had ceased, and his anger took its rightful place.

The horses of three Numidian horsemen below commanded his attention. They were strong and shirtless like their Numidian Cavalry Commander, Maharbal.

"My General! My General!" one of the approaching horsemen hailed from below.

The other four men came running onto the balcony, led by Hasdrubal Bok. "What is it?" Hasdrubal Bok said.

"The trackers have located the Celtiberians! Twenty or thirty men. Half a moon's ride!"

"Are you sure they are the ones who killed General Hamilcar!?"

The horseman placed a fist to his heart, a sign of unyielding truth or a swift death to one untrue in heart.

Hasdrubal Bok took command. "Maharbal, gather thirty of your best horsemen. Gisgo, I will also need twenty of your best trained foot soldiers."

"I will go with you, Brother," Hannibal said.

Hasdrubal Bok faced his brother-in-law and nodded in agreement. He placed one hand on Hannibal's shoulder and turned to Maharbal with an intense look.

"Blood you want, blood you shall have."

Bithynia, Asia Minor — 182 B.C.

Hannibal's arm trembled as he took another sip of wine. "I didn't realize how much I loved him until I held him in my arms. That was the only time we had ever embraced."

Scipio was still gazing out the window. "He was a dangerous man, Hannibal. Betrayal would have come eventually."

"I learned later that the Celtiberians were armed with *gladii*. I assume Hasdrubal was protecting me."

"Protecting you?" Scipio rubbed his chin.

"Yes, from myself," Hannibal said. "I was angry. I wanted revenge. At that time, any Celt would have to do."

Celtiberia, Hispania — 228 B.C.

Several Celtiberians surrounded the crackling campfires. They were of Spanish and Western European stock, dressed in an assortment of clothing, some in tunics, some in leather armor. There were a few women in the camp, and they celebrated wholeheartedly alongside the men with wine and dance. It was the sound of heavy hooves that propelled all the Celtiberians to grab their weapons and search for its source.

Out of the darkness, Maharbal and the Numidian horsemen in full-body, ghostly war paint entered the camp, trampling a few Celtiberians en route. The Celtiberians attempted to defend themselves but were no match for the precise spears of the cavalry. Carthaginian soldiers greeted any Celtiberians that fled on foot in the other direction. The Africans cut the Celtiberians to pieces.

Hannibal and Hasdrubal Bok were in the thick of the melee, and Hannibal was holding his own as a well-trained fighter. One of the Celtiberians sliced Hannibal in the abdomen with his *gladius*. The tall barbarian would have finished the kill if Hasdrubal Bok had not come to the rescue. Hasdrubal Bok removed the Celtiberian's head with one swing of his blade. He made sure that Hannibal's wound was not serious enough to warrant removing him from the ensuing battle. Once Hannibal gave him a reassuring nod, Hasdrubal Bok proceeded to the next combatant.

Hannibal was in the middle of the mayhem. He stumbled toward a woman and raised his sword for attack, but held back. He could not bring himself to slay a woman.

"Please do not kill me! Please spare my life and my child's!" The woman was on her knees begging Hannibal for mercy in her tribe's dialect. She was with child and held tightly to the round belly protruding under her robe.

Hannibal hesitated and held his wound as it began to throb in pain. Everything was blurry. His body was turning cold, and he realized that his wound was deeper than he first diagnosed. Hannibal reached out to the woman, hoping to remove her from the battlefield. However, he was too late; a spear had just struck her in the back. She fell to her death. Immediately, Maharbal reached down from his black mare and pulled the spear from the woman's body as steam flowed from his horse's nostrils.

Hannibal was overcome with pain and shock. He collapsed to the ground, engulfed by the cries of battle, and lost consciousness. It was at that moment he recalled that ominous night many years ago with his father.

Hannibal was a nine-year-old boy once more, walking the dark hallways of Hamilcar's fortress. There was crying in the distance. Hannibal followed the source of the lament to the altar room within the temple. He remembered the glow from the failing torchlight and the statue of Ba'al, a bearded warrior with ram horns, against the north wall of the large chamber. Kneeling before the small statue was Hamilcar. A single candlelight illuminated the face of the emotionally drained general. A timid Hannibal walked over and knelt beside him.

"He has spoken to me," Hamilcar mumbled.

Hannibal noticed that Hamilcar's hands were covered with blood and there was a sheep's carcass with a single hole in its belly. Blood drained into a wooden cup, some trickling along its side.

"Rome must burn for our survival," Hamilcar continued.

"They would see Carthage destroyed. Why has Ba'al forsaken me?"

Hannibal stared into his father's eyes and felt the agony in them. It ran deep.

Hamilcar grabbed the cup, drank from it and handed it to Hannibal. "You will use fire and steel. Swear before Ba'al that you will destroy Rome."

Hannibal gazed at the cup for what seemed like an eternity, then upon his father once more. "I swear before Ba'al." Hannibal drank the blood from the cup. He forced the thick liquid down his narrow throat, swallowing just enough to prevent choking.

He turned to the candle as the blood trickled from the corners of his mouth and the candlelight grew brighter. His fate was sealed with a sip of paganism.

9.

Hannibal was back in New Carthage when he stirred from his slumber. He tried to sit up, but the pain in his abdomen forced him back to the wooden, cloth-lined table. Hannibal was able to discern by the décor that he was in the airy chamber where Synhus healed men. Indeed, when his vision cleared, Synhus was looming beside him with a discerning eye.

"Rest for now." Synhus placed a hand upon the heart of Hannibal. "You lost much blood, but Ba'al watched over you."

Hannibal looked at his abdomen and observed the bandage that covered his wound. Synhus searched over his shoulder and requested in Greek for Imilce to bring the herbs. From behind Synhus approached Imilce, a beautiful, statuesque young lady with long, silky black hair, exotically alluring for a woman of such a young age. She was dressed in an inconspicuous violet robe and appeared to glide across the floor.

"I will inform Hasdrubal Bok that you have awoken." Having said that, Synhus departed.

Imilce unwrapped the bandage, and Hannibal winced with each movement. She apologized for the suffering she was causing him and Hannibal replied pleasantly in Greek. He smiled with satisfaction, partly from her beauty, partly from his self-gratification for understanding Greek. He could comprehend every soft word that flowed from her rose-colored lips, and he continued to smile. Imilce was surprised that this African warrior could speak her native tongue. She returned his smile.

"I can speak your language as well," Imilce said while blushing. "Where did you learn Greek?" She refused to raise her head. Instead, she focused on applying Hannibal's fresh bandage.

"I had a teacher. Are you impressed?"

Imilce lifted her head and secured the bandage with a thorn from dry brush. "No, I am finished."

Before Imilce could pull her hand away, Hannibal caressed her wrist. A euphoric anxiety surged through Imilce's small frame.

It dawned on Hannibal that Imilce was in fact the little girl he had encountered ten years ago. "I remember you. You were singing a song." He had never forgotten the melody, but the lyrics were still foreign to him.

Imilce reached for the goblet on the table. Gently touching Hannibal on the head, she placed the goblet to his mouth. Hannibal hesitated for a second then drank the water and immediately started coughing from the bad taste. With a stroke of her hand, Imilce wiped the excess from his lips and cheek. After Hannibal had as much as he could swallow, Imilce set the goblet down and moved toward the exit.

"I know you are from Castulo, but why are you in New Carthage?" Hannibal shouted, hoping to draw her back in.

Imilce paused at the door, and Hannibal could decipher her whisper as she walked out. "Why are you, Hannibal?"

It was the sound of her voice that followed Hannibal into another restful sleep. "Imilce."

Five years had passed before Hannibal would see Imilce again. During that time, Hannibal established himself as a warrior and a leader in the Northern Campaigns. In one attack upon a Celtiberian encampment south of Ilerda, Hannibal proved his resourcefulness to his men.

As the tribe slept during the night in their straw-roof tents, under the guise of darkness, Hannibal sent a few hundred men ahead to take up posts outside each dwelling. Upon his order, Hannibal had his Balearic slingers hurl fireballs from a distance onto the flammable tops of the tents. In a panic, the Celtiberians fled, many of them engulfed in flames. Had they known what awaited them outside, they may have decided otherwise. The men Hannibal had posted in the darkness cut the Celts to pieces as soon as they ran into view. It was a slaughter. Soon the area belonged to Hannibal, and it only cost his small army a loss of ten warriors. He was twenty-four years old.

However, it was Hasdrubal Bok who pursued doggedly Hamilcar's dream of restoring Carthage as the dominant power in the Mediterranean. Those were the days of brutality, anguish and carnage. For years they fought to bring stability to Hispania, driving the Illergetes to the Pyrenees and expanding Carthaginian rule as far south as Gades. Hasdrubal Bok would bring peace through diplomatic means. He had success with the Iberians, but one thorn remained lodged in his side, thwarting his plans—the port city known as Saguntum.

Across the *Mare Internum* in southern Latium stood Rome, the city of the gods. The spoils of the first war with Carthage revealed themselves. Pillars towered over the paved roads. Cathedrals and statues of the Roman gods climbed high above the necropolis' massive walls. There was a sense of contentment among the Roman citizens as they went about their everyday life. The construction of the stadium had begun to honor the people of Rome with games that rivaled those of Greece. Huge bricks made their way through the roadways by way of muscular henchman, hired from neighboring provinces of Etruria with Roman Senate funds.

Not far from the site dwelled the ivory walls of the playhouse where a tribune in full armor led three legionnaires down a bare corridor within the structure. It did not take them long to reach the balcony that hosted two men high above the rest of the audience watching a Greek tragedy unfold on stage.

The high-ranking officer saluted by raising his palm and whispered in the ear of the old veteran. "Consul, we've received word of Hasdrubal Bok's position."

Consul Publius Cornelius Scipio was a consul of the Roman military and the father of Scipio the Younger, later known as Scipio Africanus. This middle-aged general was Roman to the bone, and he wore his arrogance like a bright orange cape. His son Scipio the Younger sat beside him, enjoying the performance. The nineteen-year-old man had yet to develop the eyes of steel that would lead men into battle. For now, the young man was content to sit beside his father, a patriarch in a toga.

"Continue." Scipio the Elder adjusted the knot of his garment and addressed the tribune without taking his eyes off the performance.

"It seems, Consul, that the Carthaginian has successfully driven the Gaul back to the Iberus, and that there are over seventy-five thousand men in his infantry."

Scipio the Elder folded his legs with confidence and felt great satisfaction in the fact that it was he who had devised this plan. He would see it through till the final act. "Send a message to Governor Aralas in Saguntum. He may proceed with our plan."

"By your command." With a slight bow, the tribune departed.

Scipio the Younger espied his father peripherally. He was unsure what had transpired, but he knew his father all too well. His devious ways were noted on several occasions. Every moment of his childhood linked back to Sicily. It was there that his father had arisen to honorable status, having been successful in the first war with Carthage. He had even been selected as delegation leader to accept their surrender, an honor of the highest sort. Indeed, there were even plans to erect a statue of the consul before the Assembly building. Nonetheless, Publius Cornelius Scipio the Younger could see the bitterness running through his father's veins. Any mention of Carthage only drew him in closer to the point of a controlled rage.

The crowd applauded at the finale as the costumed actors below paid homage to Quintus Fabius Maximus, who was seated in the distance. Fabius had a placid appearance. He made no attempt to cover his receding hairline with a feather crest or conceal his less than flattering midsection. Fabius was a simple man but also the most powerful man in Rome, which was attested by his considerable entourage.

As Quintus Fabius Maximus and his followers stood and clapped in appreciation of the actors' rendition of The Odyssey, Scipio the Elder cocked his head and gazed unfavorably at Fabius. "I should be leading Rome." He bit the corner of his lips, ready to jump through the air and into the balcony on which Fabius stood. He would strangle him; choke the life out of the man that stood in his way to greater glory. In time. For the moment he would turn his attention to the matter westward.

"I defeated Hamilcar in Sicily. I shall finish Hasdrubal Bok in Hispania."

10.

The beautiful array of various blossoms stretched a hundred feet and was adorned with fountains that provided a sense of serenity. While picking the dead leaves off a rose bush, Imilce hummed the song that she sang as a child.

"I remember that melody," Hannibal said, purposely surprising the beautiful singer.

Startled, Imilce pricked herself with a thorn. She winced and watched the blood drop trickle down her finger. She tried to apply pressure just as Hannibal revealed himself from behind a bush. The chest plate of his armor gleamed in the sunlight.

"Look what you have done! I told you to not do that," Imilce said without facing Hannibal.

Hannibal approached Imilce and held her wounded olive-skinned hand. He moved her finger to his lips and tasted the blood. "I am sorry."

"Are you following me?" Imilce pulled her hand back and resumed tending to the rosebush. She was just over twenty-one, and every word that flowed from her lips hypnotized Hannibal.

"I heard you singing. I love to hear you sing that song."

"My mother would sing that song to me when father would go away."

"Imilce, why will you not become my wife?" The voice of defeat emanated from Hannibal's inquiry. Throughout the campaigns to the north, he had never laid with a woman, unlike his mercenary troops, who often subjugated a tribe's females with brute force. Hannibal could only think of Imilce, to obey her song and return to her with honor.

Imilce paused and let the roses she held glide onto the soil below. "I do love you."

"Then bring happiness and peace to my life. I have never enjoyed the pleasures that you would give me. I need you."

"Hannibal, Joy of Ba'al." Imilce was crying. "I fear we may never know true happiness." The tears flowed, and she wanted Hannibal to have a clear view of her emotions.

"Before father and mother were killed, they hid me in a small subterranean vault. I waited there for days, confident they would come for me. They never did. When I had the courage to finally come out, I discovered them on the floor with their throats slit." Imilce clenched her soiled hands. She was angry, but she did not want to be. "Father had more scars on him. They had tortured him for hours. Because he was a Greek merchant in Sicily, they believed that he was supplying the Romans. Maybe the Sidonian war party was looking for gold to plunder. I am not sure. Hannibal, you are a good man, but there is no such thing as a good soldier. There is no good side in war. It is evil in every way. And I could never marry a man who could not see the beauty in living." Sidonian was Greek for Carthaginian.

Hannibal knelt down and picked up the leaves that she dropped. He handed them to Imilce, cupping her hand with his. Hannibal spoke in Greek. "I am a soldier, but I still see beauty in life. And I understand what it means to lose a father."

New Carthage, Spain—220 B.C.

There was a celebration in the Grand Hall that evening. Exotic Iberian women danced to the sounds of a quick drum and flutes. Carthaginian and Numidian soldiers danced and drank. One Iberian slave held two large mugs as he approached Hasdrubal Bok, Hannibal, Maharbal, Gisgo, Synhus and Imilce, who held tightly to her newborn carefully wrapped in soft linen. He bowed and placed the mugs before Hasdrubal Bok and Hannibal then departed without taking his eyes off the floor.

"You are now a father, Hannibal! Your beautiful wife has given you a strong warrior. We drink in honor of your son," rejoiced Hasdrubal Bok as all the men at the table stood to cheer. "May Ba'al be with him." They sat.

"Will you ever have children, Brother?" Hannibal said.

Hasdrubal Bok contemplated Hannibal's question and smiled. "I have many, Brother. It is the wives I cannot keep!"

They all roared as another slave brought Hasdrubal Bok a mug.

Hannibal turned to Hasdrubal Bok. "Tell me something, Brother. How can we offer Hispania freedom from Rome's tyranny when we keep them in chains?"

Hasdrubal Bok turned to Hannibal with a menacing look then burst out laughing. Enjoying the moment, Hasdrubal Bok pranced over to dance with the women. The onlookers cheered him on until he stopped without warning. With a wave of his hand, the accompanying drum grew silent. The audience stared in anticipation.

"My brother has a son and I a nephew!" The crowd cheered. "We must also celebrate peace! For ten years, we have fought and driven the Gaul back! I shall leave for

Saguntum at dawn. There, a treaty shall be signed! Rome will know Hispania belongs to Carthage, and Carthage is forever!"

The crowd cheered even louder as Maharbal leaned over to Hannibal. "Your brother...the politician."

Hannibal was in his chambers making comical facial expressions to his infant son Giscon when there was a knock at the door.

"Enter."

Gisgo hurried in. "Hannibal!"

"Gisgo, look at Giscon. I think he grows a little every moment."

It was Gisgo's uncomfortable expression that forced Hannibal to look up. As though he held the weight of destruction upon his lips, Gisgo grunted with disdain. "Hasdrubal Bok has not returned. We have been deceived!"

Hannibal, Gisgo and about fifty horsemen raced on horseback to the walled city of Saguntum, stopping just outside the gate. Atop the wall above them stood Manicus, a muscular, rugged-looking centurion, a veteran soldier in full plate armor. Several Roman legionnaires looked down upon Hannibal as well.

"Carthaginian, why have you approached my city?" Manicus screamed.

"Four moons ago, my brother, Hasdrubal Bok, met with Governor Aralas. Since then, he and his guards have not returned. Where is my brother?"

"I am not a keeper of Carthaginians. I am unaware of your brother's whereabouts."

Some of the legionnaires chuckled.

"I want to see Aralas," Hannibal sneered.

"He is a busy man. You cannot see him. I will tell him that you wish to have a dialogue in the future. Who may I tell him is calling?" Manicus leaned forward to ensure he heard Hannibal over the strong ocean gale that was crossing the landscape.

"I am Hannibal Barca, son of Hamilcar, and I will see him now." Hannibal was at the limit of his anger. He steadied his steed, maintaining control over the powerful beast.

"You cannot enter, Hannibal Barca." Manicus replied.

"Is that so?"

"That is so." Manicus responded more firmly as the number of legionnaires on the wall increased.

Hannibal would appease him, for now. "Well then, tell Aralas that I look forward to meeting him in person."

"I shall." Manicus grew weary of pleasantries. "Now, I suggest you search for your brother elsewhere."

Hannibal grinned, tugged at his reins and galloped off.

Later that stormy evening, Hannibal and Synhus sat before the statue of Ba'al, the same sculpture beside which Hannibal and Hamilcar had once made a bond. They sat there in meditation in the candlelit room.

Synhus spoke in the ancient Phoenician tongue. "Al'iyu qarradima. To attack Saguntum would mean war with Rome."

Hannibal's immediate response was the sweat that trickled down his forehead. "He's there."

"And if so, are you prepared to go to war?"

Hannibal opened his eyes. "Yes. The Romans can never be trusted. Why could Hasdrubal not see that? Father was right. He was always right."

"Hannibal, Joy of Ba'al, you are very much like Hamilcar." Synhus smiled with his palms resting upwards.

Hannibal was drawn out of his trance and lifted himself up from the floor. "You say that as though to wound me?" Even in jest, Hannibal understood the wit of the mystic, spiteful and wicked.

"Ba'al is truth above all. As a father to a son, I will always tell you the truth."

"So much of who I am, I owe to you, Synhus. You have been almost a father to me. But alas, you are not." Hannibal spoke as though there was a listener within his heart. "I am the first son of Hamilcar Barca. I have a responsibility, and I will not shame him in death--"

"As you did in life?" interrupted Synhus, still meditating.

Hannibal was silent for a moment. "No."

"We cannot live our lives to others' expectations. You are before two paths as Gapen and Ugar have told me. Decide with your heart, and Ba'al will understand. Follow the path not provided by Ba'al, and he will extract a heavy tribute." Synhus opened his eyes.

Hannibal let his fingers stroke the ancient Phoenician writings on the obelisk. "I can only choose the path before me. If my brother is alive, I must bring him home."

11.

The Carthaginian army's siege engines and battering rams assaulted the fortified city of Saguntum as soldiers climbed the storming towers. Many men were cut down by pila and boulders, falling to their deaths. Not far from the siege stood Hannibal's camp where Hannibal, Maharbal and Gisgo sat upon their steeds, watching the battle unfold. Behind them waited reserve soldiers and the Numidian cavalry.

Watching his soldiers cry out in agony, Gisgo reacted with consternation. "We're losing many soldiers, Hannibal. The gate is too strong. They may not--"

Almost unaware of his first officer, the young general studied the battle before him. "In time. In time."

A Numidian horseman rode up from behind. "They are here, General!"

"Your cavalry can ride anything, is that right?" Hannibal smiled at Maharbal.

Perplexed, Maharbal turned to him. "My cavalry can ride the wind."

Hannibal followed the horseman across the vast plain until they reached a caravan of Carthaginian soldiers followed by approximately thirty elephants. In front were three men in full armor on horseback. They leaped off their mounts and sprinted toward Hannibal. Hannibal jumped off his steed and ran to meet them.

They were in Hispania at last. Many nights had come to

a close when Hannibal thought of his beloved brothers, who were now in his gaze once again: Mago, Hasdrubal and Hanno. They were obviously much older than he remembered. Mago had grown taller but was still the shortest. Hasdrubal was very tall but thin. Hanno's baby fat had transformed into muscle. He was a big man. Although they wanted to share an embrace, a cloud of uneasiness hung over their gathering. They stood there, wondering what words they would utter after so many years. It was Hannibal who broke the silence.

"Mago, Hasdrubal and Hanno, it is good to see you, Brothers. How is mother?"

The corners of Mago's mouth curled downward. "Not well since Father died."

Hanno made light of the tense moment immediately by grabbing Hannibal in a headlock. "We all missed you, Older Brother."

"Hanno, you may be bigger, but I can still out-wrestle you," Hannibal said with a chuckle.

"I made you something." Hasdrubal gave Hannibal a painting of a lion beside a red river.

Hannibal was surprised but tempered his emotions with appreciation. "How did you know, Hasdrubal?"

Hasdrubal grasped Hannibal's shoulder. "I heard you when you slept."

"I will keep it close to my heart." Hannibal returned Hasdrubal's embrace.

"My art is heralded throughout all of Greece." To Hannibal, Hasdrubal's boasts were not a sign of arrogance; they were merely his younger brother's way of conveying some useful information to his siblings. Hannibal nodded with a prideful grin.

Hanno felt that he too was also obligated to share his triumphs. "I am the champion wrestler of Carthage!"

"Is that so?" Hannibal shouted.

"The Romans will regret what they did to our father, right Hannibal?"

Hannibal knew that Hasdrubal was still as direct as he had been twenty years ago. "And for what they did to Hasdrubal Bok."

"Hasdrubal Bok was weak. He did not have Barca blood."

"He was still our brother, Mago."

"No brother of mine," Mago said under his breath.

Hannibal realized Mago embodied the same rage he possessed as a child, pain and abandonment. Yet he hadn't the time to dwell on childhood differences. There were greater concerns facing the Carthaginians. Hannibal admired the line of elephants. "They are fine animals."

"What will you do with them, Hannibal?" Hanno said.

""We are together again." Hannibal placed his hand on Hanno's shoulder. "That is the first key."

As Hannibal besieged Saguntum, Aralas shared a large table of fruit and grain delights with several of Saguntum's patricians within the city's walls. They drank wine and chortled in joyous celebration of their recent gains in wealth. Manicus entered the room.

"Hannibal has broken off his attack and has fallen back. Should we follow, Governor?"

Aralas stood, stumbling from the wine. "So, the son of Hamilcar has given up!"

"We have lost many legionnaires and defenses, Governor. If we move offensively, we can divert--"

Aralas's obstinate personality revealed itself. "No! They too are weakened. Let their futility recommence at dawn."

It was dark with the exception of a few torches. Two legionnaires paced the gate, staring down at some of Saguntum's citizens outside the protective wall, pillaging the Carthaginian army's dead. Meanwhile, Aralas and his guests continued their celebration while looking at a large map of Spain placed on the table.

"Once we crush the Carthaginians, I shall control all of Hispania," Aralas said. "Which means more land for you, my friends."

The men rejoiced until they were interrupted by a repetitive trembling of the ground. The loud rattle shook their half-filled wineglasses.

Manicus, dressed in tunic and robe, hurried from his quarters toward the wall. He maintained his footing, stumbling with every tremor that shook the fortress grounds. Immediately, a tribune met him.

"What is it?" Manicus shouted to the sentry above.

"A landshake!"

"A landshake in Hispania?"

Several legionnaires scurried toward the wall amidst the mayhem. They stumbled as the tremors became louder and more intense, shattering the supporting wood shafts bracing the gate. One legionnaire on the wall was able to maintain his balance and stare out into the dark landscape beyond the city. He squinted then his jaw dropped and eyes widened. He turned and screamed before the great impact.

"Elephants!"

The gate came crashing down by the unstoppable force

of two of the massive animals, one mounted by Maharbal and the other by a Numidian horseman.

Manicus darted for his tent to arm himself. "Legionnaires! Hannibal ad portas!"

The elephants trampled the screaming legionnaires. They were followed by hundreds of Carthaginians rushing into the compound, led by Hannibal on foot. Mago and Hanno were beside him initially, but they soon dispersed, slashing their way through the weaker, less armored legionnaires.

Hannibal, with sword and spear, moved through the disorganized legionnaires like a man possessed, blood splashing on his armor. He had dismembered three men before Manicus stood twenty feet in front of him.

Manicus had a look of desperation. He searched for a soldier to defend him, but there were none around. Welding a *gladius*, he rushed Hannibal.

Hannibal fell to one knee, drove his sword into the dirt and launched his spear at Manicus. It pierced the Roman officer in the chest, through and through. Manicus fell, coughing up blood. Satisfied that Manicus was no more, Hannibal's head swiveled in search of his main objective. "Find Aralas!"

Aralas began gathering all the personal wealth he could carry. Several coins and jewels slipped through his grasp before reaching the sack readied for transport. His greed remained a driving force, even when faced with panic.

A young legionnaire stood with him, trembling from the screams he heard coming from outside the chamber. Then came silence. The legionnaire unsheathed his *gladius*. His heartbeat filled his ears, muffling all other sounds.

Crash.

The door shattered and several Carthaginian soldiers entered. The legionnaire attempted to defend himself and Aralas but was quickly cut to pieces by the Carthaginians. After witnessing the legionnaire's fate, Aralas darted to a secret passage with his sack. He reached the stone-panel entrance of the passage but stopped in utter fear and stumbled to his knees. A blood-covered Hannibal, followed by Mago and Hanno, exited the secret passage and loomed large over the fleeing governor.

Aralas cried out like a child awaiting his punishment. "Have mercy! Please have mercy!"

Hannibal clenched the governor by his throat. "Where is my brother?" Hannibal drew his sword.

Aralas continued to plead for his life. "In the dungeon! Listen, take the--"

Before Aralas could finish his offering, Hannibal released his hold and sliced Aralas's throat. The brothers watched as Aralas gasped for air. He soon fell into a pool of blood. In a state of numb consciousness and spiritual clarity, Hannibal stepped over Aralas's corpse and left the room. The brothers followed after Mago took the opportunity to spit on Aralas's body as he departed.

Hannibal unlocked the heavy wooden door, letting light into the damp, rat-infested cell located deep within the dungeon. Hannibal stepped in and saw a dark shadow hanging from the wall. He approached Hasdrubal Bok slowly, who was chained at the wrists. His limp body was beaten and dark, coagulated blood covered adhered to his flesh.

Hannibal unsheathed his sword and struck the chains until they broke. Dropping his weapon, he grabbed hold of the lifeless Hasdrubal Bok and lowered him down. Hannibal remembered Hamilcar's death and held on tightly to his surrogate brother. Gisgo entered the room. Upon witnessing the inevitable demise of Hasdrubal Bok, he was drawn to tears. Gisgo wiped his cheek and placed a hand on Hannibal's shoulder. "What of the city?"

"Burn it." Hannibal carefully lifted Hasdrubal Bok over his shoulder.

Gisgo took a deep breath. "And the women and children?" Gisgo had never witnessed the rage that was now contorting Hannibal's lips and turning his eyes into narrow slits. He knew Hannibal's final two words before leaving with Hasdrubal Bok would endure beyond that moment.

"Burn it!"

Carthage, Africa—218 B.C.

In the dimly lit chamber where Hamilcar once stood, the interior council chamber of the Suffete was the center point of tension. The clanking of boots and armor echoed as the plump, toga-clad Roman ambassador, accompanied by four legionnaires and a centurion, approached the Suffete seated behind the stone podium. Senators Cobo and Bragibas were twenty years older but nevertheless still alive and in command. The ambassador was brought to a halt by a wall of Carthaginian guards.

"Good morning, Ambassador," Bragibas offered.

"You have broken the treaty," the ambassador replied.

"Broken the treaty?" Bragibas folded his arms.

"It is Rome who has broken the treaty." Cobo pointed with indignation. "Saguntum was never a condition that we discussed. No Romans were allowed in Hispania."

The ambassador stood strong to the hoots that followed

Cobo's response. "Nevertheless, you have a murderous rebel running wild in Hispania. We demand retribution."

"What form shall this retribution take?" Senator Bragibas demanded.

"The people of Rome demand the immediate surrender of Hannibal Barca."

The Suffete chortled in unison.

"Rome may demand nothing of Carthage. Instead, Rome must explain its violation, Ambassador," Bragibas shouted.

The Suffete grunted in agreement as the ambassador stepped to within a few feet of the massive podium. He clenched the cloth of his toga with both hands to symbolize the proposal he presented.

"Your decision today is simple. In this hand, I bring the peace our two lands have enjoyed," the ambassador said, referring to his left hand then to his right. "In the other, I bring a war that you can never fathom. Which do you choose?"

The Suffete was silent as the men looked to one another for reactions and guidance. Senator Cobo's face displayed its usual snarl. "Let Rome choose."

The ambassador maintained his cold persona and released the hold of the right side of his toga. "Then war it is!"

"Then war it is," barked Senator Cobo.

The Suffete cheered as the ambassador and his escort departed the chamber. However, Senator Bragibas did not. He lowered his head and closed his eyes in regret.

Once again, death and carnage had found their place in the annals of Carthaginian lore.

12.

Hannibal, Hanno, Mago, Hasdrubal, Gisgo and Maharbal searched for a strategy using the map of the Mediterranean spread across the table. It was Mago who directed everyone's attention to the island of Corsica.

"If we land our ships to the west, we should have Corsica by next autumn."

"From there, a direct path to Rome. Very good," Gisgo said.

Hasdrubal did not concur with the two officers. "Good enough to be the obvious move. The Romans will probably have every eastward port covered, from Corsica to Sardinia."

"Maybe, we should launch from Carthage, move north into Sicily?" offered Hanno.

"Also, obvious."

"Everywhere is obvious." Gisgo agreed with Hasdrubal's conclusion.

"Yes--"

"And no." Hannibal focused the men's attention to the northern lands on the map. Needless to say, the men were dumbfounded. "They own the sea," Hannibal continued. "So we will attack by land."

Mago shrugged, assuming Hannibal's plan was the obvious decision. "Of course, but we must control the waters for suitable landings."

"There will be no landing." Hannibal's index finger tracked the invisible line flowing over lands that are known today as France, Switzerland and Italy. "We will attack from the north by moving through the Alps and Cisalpine Gaul."

Gisgo felt that it was his responsibility to question the illogical commands of his leader. He did so with Hamilcar, and Hannibal was no different. "Through the mountains? Even if we do not perish from the mountains, the Gaul tribes will cut us to pieces. And if by some miracle we survive that, Rome is heavily fortified."

"Still fearful of water, Brother?" Mago said.

Hannibal smirked at Mago's remark and continued his assessment of the battle at hand. "I have already sent messengers to the tribes. The Vicontii and the Tricorii will not interfere, nor will the Allobroges and the Boii."

"Even so, Brother, to attack Rome directly is suicide," Mago said in a more serious tone.

Hannibal thought for a brief moment and sauntered away from the men.

"Is it? Over the years, I have learned much from Father. He once said that Rome is more of a philosophy than a society. The people of Etruria must see firsthand that not even Rome can protect them from destruction. You break their spirit, you cripple Rome...and so goes the Roman threat."

"I understand." Gisgo shined with awareness.

"Foolhardy perhaps, but it is certainly not the obvious strategy," Hasdrubal said.

"Let us be stronger than the mountains," bellowed Maharbal.

Hannibal smiled and returned to the men. "Gisgo, you are the rightful commander now."

Gisgo was honored that Hannibal considered his notion of pride. "No, Hannibal. You have the respect of the men and myself. They know you are a brave soldier and a very capable commander. It is as though Hamilcar brought you to Hispania so many years ago for this very moment. You will lead now, General."

"Agreed," Maharbal said. "Long live the boy general."

"I will honor you." Hannibal acknowledged Gisgo's loyalty with a humble nod and without hesitation moved forward with tactical planning. "Hasdrubal, you will stay in Hispania and ensure that our navy is ready when the time comes."

Hasdrubal approached Hannibal in contempt. "I will not be left behind. You need me with you."

"Hannibal is right, Hasdrubal," Mago said.

Hasdrubal became infuriated. "I can wield a sword as well as a brush." He smashed his hand on the table beneath him.

Hannibal patted Hasdrubal on the shoulder. "Brother, I need a sound mind to protect our interests in Hispania. And only a brother can protect my family. Do that for me, Brother."

Hasdrubal's body language conceded. "I hope Ba'al is with you, Hannibal."

"I hope he is with us all," Hannibal said, "for it will not end until Rome is no more."

Hannibal remembered the deaths of Hamilcar and Hasdrubal Bok, the lessons he had learned from them, and the wisdom he hoped that Synhus had passed on to him. Part of him wallowed in the realm of fear. He had fought in many battles, but this fear felt like none he had ever experienced. It was the fear that an entire people depended on the decisions he made from that moment on.

Imilce handed Giscon to Hannibal. Careful not to let his bronze-plate leather armor harm the first-born and heir to the

Barca name, Hannibal rubbed his small head gently. He gazed at his beautiful wife, who smiled back with watery eyes. He then kissed the infant and handed him back to Imilce. Hannibal approached the open balcony and took a deep breath, gazing at the moving clouds above for some guidance. Gradually, he walked out onto the balcony.

Outside the fortress, thousands of soldiers—Iberians, Africans, Numidians, Ligurians and Gaul in rank and file—had gathered, anxiously awaiting the appearance of Hannibal, the new leader of Hispania. The Iberian, Greek and Sicilian slaves who were captured in conquest were also in the assembly, ready to hear his words. Hannibal's eyes found those of his trusted officers Maharbal, Gisgo and Synhus, and his brothers Hanno, Hasdrubal and Mago. He raised his hand and the crowd grew silent. Only the waves crashing against the shore could be heard, and Hannibal took a moment to savor the stillness. As Hannibal spoke, several translators called out his words to the crowd in their respective native tongues.

"I ask you for open eyes, open ears and open hearts. How can I fight the Roman threat if I do not abide by the truths I know are right?

Slaves, you are the servants of Carthage no longer. You are now part of us, free to go to your homelands if you choose. Or, you can join the brave soldiers before me who will not see their dreams squashed at the heels of Roman dominance any longer. I invite you to be allies in the destruction of the greater glory of Rome!"

The slaves were amazed by what they had just heard. Both men and women were brought to tears as soldiers scattered to place assorted weaponry before the feet of the captured people. Many of the men kissed their loved ones and began donning the weapons.

Hannibal continued. "The Romans have demanded that my brothers and I surrender to them, immediately. So I responded, send a ship to take us to Rome, and I willingly submit."

Murmurs of surprise rippled through the crowd.

"Of course, they must understand that I have over a hundred thousand brothers. It may take them many years to build a ship that large."

The soldiers roared in laughter as the translations continued to funnel through.

"The journey ahead is a difficult one, but not impossible. Alexander conquered the Alps, and so shall we. For many of you, the mountains are not to be feared; you will simply be returning to the place you knew as a child. Despite the many Gaul allies we have made along the Rhone, many of you will find the road ahead a challenge, one that will determine not only what kind of soldier you are, but more importantly, what kind of man you are." Hannibal paused to gaze over the men below him. "But I promise you this. Every man who survives this journey will be rewarded with riches beyond his wildest dreams and the heraldry that comes from it. He will have before him the greatest treasure of all...the city of Rome itself!"

A thunderous cheer erupted.

"Rome believes that we will attack by sea. They believe seafarers cannot be good soldiers. To attack by land would be foolish!" Hannibal then revealed his charismatic grin that exuded confidence. "What separates foolishness from bravery is victory. May Ba'al be at our backs."

The soldiers chanted their battle cries in support of their general, raising their weapons to the sky.

Upon reaching the dawn of the eighth moon passing, the Carthaginian army embarked from New Carthage. Across the grassy plains, Hannibal's army was a mile long. The caravan was lead by 37 elephants and followed by one hundred thousand infantry and cavalry, pack animals towing supplies, siege engines, battering rams and the bloodthirsty wrath that flowed through the veins of Hannibal Barca. He sat alone with the mahout in the tower on top of the lead elephant, Surus, wondering if Hamilcar watched over him from beside the throne of Ba'al.

13.

Bithynia, Asia Minor—182 B.C.

Hannibal lifted his bloodied hand and checked his wound, enjoying another sip of wine. For a brief moment, Scipio the Younger studied Hannibal from the chair across from the Carthaginian.

"And from there, I marched on to pursue the dream my father had held on to for so long," Hannibal said, fighting the desire to hunch over in agony.

"A bold decision to choose land over sea." Though his remark may have been directed to Hannibal's face, Scipio's vision followed the leaking blood seeping through Hannibal's fingers.

"But time was not on my side." Hannibal replied. "I had to be past the Pyrenees before your father's legion landed."

"A task that you accomplished very easily."

Hannibal was taken aback by Scipio's bold display of overconfidence. "It was a difficult task indeed. To besiege a citadel is one matter, but to lead over a hundred thousand soldiers from different lands across vast mountains is another."

Scipio recalled his younger days alongside his father. "In his logs, my father noted that many villages welcomed you. Your learning of Greek proved instrumental in your alliance with Emporion."

Remembering that march, Hannibal could only let out a smile of imitation.

"I wish the Volcae shared your optimism."

Rhone River, Gaul—218 B.C.

Hundreds of spears hurled from the wooded bank opposite them whistled through the air, picking off Hannibal's soldiers before they could even secure themselves upon their man-made rafts to cross the tumultuous Rhone. Their shields seemed useless, and soon the blood of many dead Iberians and Africans flooded the river crimson. Those with armor sunk and drowned to the bottom, and those without armor floated lifelessly, projectiles protruding from their exposed flesh, soldiers who were frantically trying to board their rafts. The warriors who survived their wounds bellowed in pain, amplifying the din of the battle. On horseback with sword drawn, Gisgo pressed his men to continue forward, occasionally repelling a flying spear with his blade.

"Secure the rafts before loading! Let us pass these savages, men!"

Hannibal's rage was directed at the Volcae, Gallic tribesmen who were defending their land fearlessly. They numbered in the hundreds, wore heavy unkempt beards and animal skin fur, and uttered bloodcurdling battle cries as they unleashed their deadly swarm of weapons upon Hannibal's men. One of their victims, an Iberian, became caught in the current and floated toward the Gaul. Before he could attempt to defend himself with his rusty blade, he was ambushed by several Gaul, who proceeded to reign their clubs upon his hapless head. His screams served only to further unnerve the dispirited Carthaginian forces.

Some distance away, Hannibal, dressed in his tunic with breastplate, overlooked the battle by the river while the bare-chested Maharbal sat upon his horse. As he surveyed the carnage below, Hannibal's heart was overcome with despair. In the distance, Synhus was attending to the returning wounded who had miraculously survived the ordeal. A reserve force of cavalry and infantry awaited orders behind the mounted commanders.

Accompanied by one Iberian officer and one Carthaginian soldier, Mago galloped up to the two men. He controlled his heavy breathing long enough to report on the slaughter.

"We haven't a chance, Brother! The men are being speared before they even reach their rafts! What do you want me to do?"

"Continue the assault," Hannibal said.

Mago was aghast. "Brother, did you not hear what I have said? The current is too strong! The men are dying needlessly!"

Hannibal stared into Mago's eyes. "Mago, do as I command. Tell Gisgo to maintain the battle. Commit a few soldiers at a time."

"Hannibal--"

"Do as I command! Now!"

Almost biting his lip off, Mago yanked his horse toward the battlefield and rode off, followed by the two soldiers. Soon after, Hanno approached on horseback.

"The rafts are complete, Brother."

Hannibal's cheek fluttered as he nodded with approval. "Maharbal, have the mahouts move the elephants up river."

Maharbal pressed Hannibal to clarify the reasoning behind this command. "What good are elephants on the

Rhone?"

"Something I once read," Hannibal shouted as he snapped his reins and quickly rode away.

Maharbal could only shake his head. "I am commanded by a scroll?" He kicked his horse and rode off in full gallop toward the river below, followed by Hanno.

Maharbal set aside his qualms and dutifully implemented his commander's orders. Soon thousands of Numidian cavalry with their horses and elephants were floating across the river on massive log rafts. The vessels reached some thirty feet in length and were covered with soil. Most held one elephant and its mahout, while the others were reserved for the horsemen and their steeds. Hannibal boarded a raft that carried Surus and attempted to console the elephant with gentle strokes across its belly. Maharbal held the reins of his horse on an adjacent craft. He reached down and sifted some of the raised soil between his hardened hands.

"Why the elephants, Hannibal?"

Hannibal cupped his hands around his mouth to amplify his words. "To break the current for the main force south."

Maharbal nodded with approval. "The soil is very nice!"

"Without the earth beneath their feet, the elephants would believe that they were on water and panic!"

"And what of Numidians who panic?" Maharbal shouted.

"I say, learn to swim, my friend!"

Maharbal gave Hannibal his tender snarl.

Moments later, further down river, a flaming arrow was launched into the sky. Gisgo dismounted his horse and leapt into the waters beside several other soldiers.

Gisgo addressed his troops. "Attack!" The splash created by the wave of soldiers entering the water elicited an immediate volley of metal-tipped spears from the Volcae. Because the current had slowed considerably, the Carthaginian soldiers had an easy time retreating to their rafts where they were able to protect themselves with their shields. As the Carthaginians neared the other side of the river, the Volcae lined the coast in a defensive posture, their swords were drawn, waiting for the approaching rafts.

The ears of the Volcae warriors perked up at the sound of the thundering, fast-approaching hooves of the bare-chested Numidian horsemen. The cavalry, led by Hannibal, Maharbal and Hanno, slashed without mercy all that stood in their way. Hanno dismounted and cut down two Volcae warriors with his broadsword. One of his victims made a feeble attempt to retaliate, but the massive Hanno disposed of the assailant with a quick, neck-snapping headlock.

By this point, Gisgo, Mago and their men had made it to shore and were repelling the bewildered Volcae. Mago hacked off the arm off a Volcae fighter with his blade while Hanno eviscerated another man with a blunt, determined thrust. Realizing their futility against the Carthaginian forces, the Volcae fled for their lives into the woods. The Carthaginian army did not give chase, but raised their weapons in victory.

Hannibal stood alone with sword drawn and dripping in blood. He wiped the sweat off his brow as Maharbal approached him.

"Gather the weapons left behind."

Maharbal's eyes pierced through the fog of war, his body stained crimson from the battle. "Should we give chase?"

Hannibal surveyed the casualties suffered by both armies, the dead lying on the shore and the wounded, many of whom were still writhing about in pain. "No. It will not be long

99

before the Romans are on our heels."

Maharbal nodded and began instructing the men to gather whatever they could carry, including their comrades in arms. Hannibal approached an exhausted Mago, who was leaning against a tree. Mago was traumatized by the horrors of battle. Hannibal consoled him by holding the top of his head and grinning.

"It is different from the tournaments in Carthage."

"Yes," Mago muttered as a tear streaked down his cheek..

"You did fine."

Mago was unable to look Hannibal in the eyes. Hannibal did not wish to subject his siblings to further mortal dangers, but he knew he could not invade Rome without them. He closed his eyes and accepted the anguish.

14.

Scipio the Elder's legion sailed from Ostia and arrived at the Roman port city of Massilia, just south of Gaul territory. Legionaries and horsemen disembarked from their quinqueremes and unloaded their supplies. Scipio walked down the ramp of the ship, followed by an entourage of tribunes in full armor. The Roman consul was nauseous and swaying as he walked. A young aedile, or administrative officer, greeted him promptly with a fist-to-heart salute.

"I am pleased that the gods have offered you safe passage to Massilia, Consul."

"The oracle was not very empathetic to the sea--" Before he could finish his sentence, Scipio resisted the impulse to vomit. One of the young tribunes approached Scipio to keep him from tipping over, only to be pushed away by the older man.

"The consul has developed a bout of sea sickness. Where is your infirmary?" the tribune demanded.

"We have no time for sickness," Scipio protested.

Seizing the opportunity to gain the favor of the consul, the aedile recounted his accomplishments. "We have dispatched a cavalry unit to track the Carthaginians."

Scipio coughed heavily. "Very good. Answer me this." Scipio wagged his finger and beckoned the officer to come closer. The aedile leaned forward to ensure that he heard his commander's every word. "What of the--" Choking on his words, Scipio proceeded to soak the officer's fine tunic with vomit. The consul grunted a couple of times before being carried away by two of the tribunes.

The tribune took the opportunity to revel in the aedile's misfortune. "I warned you."

Hannibal tossed and turned in his tent. He was in the throes of another nightmare. The sweat poured down his cheeks and his eyelids fluttered. He awoke, gasping for air, his tunic drenched in perspiration. He checked his heart to make sure it was still beating. As Hannibal surveyed his surroundings, he noticed a single flickering candle nearing its end at the edge of his bedding, along with a man who was regarding him from inside the shadows of the entrance.

"Mago?" Hannibal squinted in an attempt to make out the dusky image.

Mago remained by the door and did not enter. "The men will be ready at sunlight. That is all."

"Thank you, Brother," Hannibal said.

Mago nodded and began to depart, but Hannibal called out and beckoned him to stay. Mago looked over his shoulder. "Yes, Older Brother?"

"Tell me of Mother."

"She misses you very much," Mago answered softly.

"I had no choice. I hope she understood that."

"Mother only wishes you to be well and to return home safely."

To return home, Hannibal thought to himself.

Mago shut his eyes and remembered the days of their youth. "We are happy for you. We have sometimes been jealous that Father chose only you, but perhaps we were the fortunate ones after all. You had to watch our father die."

Hannibal's eyes watered from despair. "My brothers are everything to me. We will have our vengeance."

"We know." Mago became more animated as he moved closer to Hannibal.

"For many years, I did not understand what had filled our father's heart," Hannibal confessed to his brother. "I once believed that Carthage and Rome could exist as two great lands."

Mago pointed a single finger at Hannibal. "It is possible, Brother."

"There can never be two male lions in the same pack. Only one," Hannibal said.

The tone and tempo of Mago's speech heightened considerably. "You sound just like Father. Has not the Barca family suffered enough? We cannot trust the Suffete. They will betray us, just as they did Father."

"I expect it to be over before they have a chance," Hannibal said, flush with confidence.

Mago was not in agreement with Hannibal's decision. "We have avenged Father's death. But now you are following the same foolish path as he."

Hannibal sat up and came face to face with his brother. Hannibal placed his hand on his sword's hilt. "You will not disrespect Father."

Mago rose to the challenge and entered Hannibal's tent. "He tore us apart, Hannibal. And he continues to do so today. I will fight with you, Brother, but I question what we are fighting for."

"They killed Father. They killed him in the most dishonorable way possible. All he ever wanted was to protect us! I will fulfill his dream. We owe him that much, do we not?"

"I cannot say." Mago turned away in frustration and walked out of the tent. "I never knew the man."

Spread across the open, sun-beaten field of the Vocontii area, east of the Rhone, Scipio and his legion stood in battle array. Scipio sat proudly on his horse, bronze helmet and plate armor glittering under the midday sun. The sickness had passed and he was eager to engage Hannibal as soon as mortally possible. The aedile who rode beside him reassured his commander at every turn.

"The cavalry scouts reported that they engaged the Carthaginians just over that hill. They should soon be returning to their position, Consul."

"Which means that Hannibal knows that we are here." Scipio's unforgiving eyes scanned the terrain, half expecting the deceptive Carthaginian to leap out from behind a large stone that lay at the edge of the surrounding forest.

"Our soldiers confronted some of his cavalry, but bravely drove them back. I'm sure it was spectacular."

Scipio gave the aedile a discerning look. "I'm sure Hannibal was spying on us just as we were on him."

"Yes, Consul," The aedile nodded and remained silent.

Scipio stroked the mane of his horse while inspecting the soldiers before him. "His next move will be to move south into Massilia. We will be waiting. Prey to Saturn that your Gaul ally does not betray us, Aedile."

"I assure you, Consul, everything is in place."

Three approaching Roman horsemen drew their attention. The party was led by a centurion, who dismounted his horse and saluted Scipio. The soldiers' battle-scarred armor and exhausted appearance foretold the outcome of the account they were about to present.

"Report for the consul," shouted the centurion.

"Proceed," Scipio replied.

The young officer brushed his soiled hair and adjusted his breastplate in an effort to make himself presentable. "We engaged several of their Numidians and suffered heavy casualties."

"What is the position of the main army?"

"They were not there, Consul."

"What?" Scipio had not expected an entire army to disappear.

"The main army was not --"

"I heard you, Centurion," Scipio screamed before the trembling Roman officer. The legionnaires within earshot dared not divert their gaze to view the interrogation. "What do you mean they were not there?"

"They are several days eastward. The Numidians were just a decoy, Consul."

Scipio shuttered with dismay, struggling to comprehend how a nightmare scenario like this could have come to pass. It took a moment for the commander to calculate the Carthaginian's next move, but he realized that his decision to block the port nearest to Rome had been a horrible miscalculation.

"That bastard! That bastard! He is going into the Alps. Which means he is headed for Rome." Scipio turned his horse around. "Back to Massilia! We will meet him at the other end of the Alps before he has a chance to march to Rome."

"Very good plan, Consul. I will--"

Scipio the Elder pointed at the aedile. "You will make sure that the Volcae do not scavenge the fallen horsemen."

The officer's eyes widened and his heart raced with fear. "But Consul, the Volcae are not especially fond of us."

"That is your problem, Aedile."

Hannibal's army marched through a narrow, rocky passage at the feet of the Alps, which the local inhabitants referred to as the Col de Grimone. On their left loomed a mighty alpine mountain, and on their right lay the majestic valley floor hundreds of feet below. The Allobroge Gaul controlled this region and ruthlessly attacked any trespassers who dared entered. Of course, the Carthaginians were no exception.

Without warning, a thunderous cavalcade of boulders came crashing down on the Carthaginian column, and the cries of soldiers being crushed or knocked over the narrow cliff filled the air. The elephants trumpeted wildly as they too were cast over the precipice, adding to the panic of the infantrymen. Arrows from the Gaul above pierced the flesh of Iberians, Carthaginians, Celtiberians and captive Gaul alike. The Ligurian archers attempted to return fire, but some were cut down before they even had a chance cock their bows.

Hanno, Gisgo and Mago waived the men on, trying to bring order to the chaos. Using his above-average strength, Hanno helped several soldiers keep an ox cart from falling over the cliff. Amidst the confusion, Hanno did not realize that an arrow had zipped through the air and punctured his upper back. He winced and crawled for cover. Before he knew it, a boulder tumbled down toward him, forcing him to spin off the cliff.

On a hill overlooking the skirmish, Hannibal and Maharbal on horseback observed the battle below. The bulk of the Numidian cavalry was behind them. He listened to the rhythmic chants of Synhus, who with legs folded underneath him sat atop a rock gazing up to the bright sun above.

Hannibal turned to the mystical elder. "Will Ba'al offer us any good fortunes?"

Synhus raised his hand to block the sun from his eyes. "It is difficult to say. Perhaps."

"Perhaps? What good are you?" snarled Maharbal.

"Of course, when you're high enough, Ba'al shines for everyone," Synhus replied. "Whether Ba'al is with us depends on us. He only allows for the situation to be equally fair."

Maharbal chuckled in his deep, gritty intonation with satisfaction. "Your god is the most useless god that I have ever encountered. How lazy can he be?"

"He is almost asleep at times." Hannibal drew his sword and kicked his horse in the midsection. Followed by the Numidians, he raced down the embankment.

The Allobroges concentrated above the Carthaginian column were taken by complete surprise at the arrival of the cavalry. The Numidians launched their javelins at the unsuspecting Gaul. The spears penetrated the barbarians, who fell as a result, some of them down to the Carthaginian column below. Hannibal launched his javelin and caught a Gaul warrior in the chest. Then in mid-gallop, he dismounted his steed and ran into the thick of the melee. He unsheathed his sword and with exemplary dexterity, proceeded to thrust it upwards and downwards as Gallic blood splattered on his armor.

Maharbal knocked several Gaul down to the Carthaginian army below with his javelin. Each barbarian he felled elicited a cheer from the soldiers below and brought a smile to Maharbal's face. In a frenzy, a Gaul fighter rushed Maharbal. With ease, Maharbal spun his horse around and knocked the soldier to the ground. He then hurled his javelin at the man's throat, pinning him to the hard soil. The Gaul coughed and choked on his own blood as Maharbal circled about and then removed his impaled javelin from his assailant's corpse.

It was Hannibal who faced the fiercest of the Gaul warriors. The massive, hairy man must have stood seven feet tall, and he swung a huge battle-ax effortlessly. Hannibal stared him down, not intimidated by his earsplitting battle cry. The Gaul charged forward, swinging his axe overhead, passing it from hand to hand. Suddenly, a hazy film covered Hannibal's eyes so that he could only make out the dark shape of the huge, axe-wielding man charging toward him. Hannibal ducked and rolled to the left, evading the first blow. Another swing came, and Hannibal rolled to the right, again eluding the weapon. But the Gaul recovered and struck downward with ferocity. Hannibal's only recourse was to use his sword as a shield. The giant Gaul's heavy iron axe repelled Hannibal's blade into Hannibal, causing a gash on his shoulder. Hannibal cried out in excruciating pain. The Gaul raised his battle-ax overhead, ready to split the supine Hannibal in half with a furious deathblow. At the last moment, Hannibal saw the blurry weapon coming toward his chest and rolled to his right. The blade of the battle-ax buried itself into the earth. Hannibal seized this window of opportunity and jabbed his sword into the giant's scrotum, dropping him to his knees. Mouthing a silent scream, the mighty Gaul fell like a teetering redwood. Hannibal lifted himself up and stumbled toward Maharbal, who was seated on his horse. Maharbal gave Hannibal a stern glare.

"You killed a chief. How does it feel?"

Hannibal held his wound and gazed up at Maharbal and then at his hazy surroundings. As the remaining Gaul fled in a panic, Hannibal found a rock to sit on and surveyed the wounded and the dead. In Hannibal's bleary eyes, the bloody bodies seemed to blend together. He rested his head on his bloodstained hand, as flashes of past nightmares replayed in his head.

Down below, as the conquering Carthaginians hacked away at the wounded Gaul, Mago and Gisgo bolted over to see if Hanno had fallen over the cliff. They looked over to see Hanno hanging by both hands on a depression in the mountain some ten feet below the edge. Blood flowed down his back, and he was exhausted from hanging on for dear life. Pebbles trickled down to the valley hundreds of feet below.

"Hanno!" Mago was elated to discover that his brother was still alive.

"Hanno, are you okay?" Gisgo shouted.

"What?" Hanno had just enough strength to shoot Gisgo an exasperated look.

"Hold on, Brother, we will help you!" Mago ran off to find something to help lift Hanno to safety.

"Hang on, Hanno!" Gisgo said.

"My hands are slipping!" Hanno grumbled in exhaustion.

Mago returned with a heavy rope and created a slipknot and lasso. He then lowered the line and looped the lasso under Hanno's feet. Mago and Gisgo then lifted the cord until it tightened around Hanno's underarms and chest, just as he released his grip.

The force of the falling Hanno dragged Mago and Gisgo dangerously to the edge, almost pulling them over. Fortunately, they were able to gain their footing and were soon helped by two Iberian soldiers. Using all the strength they could muster, the four men stepped backwards and struggled in-inch-by-inch to lift Hanno closer to the top.

"You know, Hanno, you're a fat bastard!" Mago said.

"Mago!" Hanno was not amused.

"Hold on!" Mago laughed as he strained to pull Hanno higher. He made light of the situation because he felt that they had a firm grasp of Hanno.

"Hurry!" Hanno pleaded.

It was at this moment that the rope snapped. The unleashed energy drove Mago, Gisgo and the Iberians into the dirt. They listened to Hanno's horrific last cries as he plummeted to the valley below.

Gisgo hopped up and darted to the edge of the cliff while Mago gazed at the limp rope in disbelief.

15.

Bithynia, Asia Minor—182 B.C.

Scipio the Younger reached across the table for Hannibal's wine carafe, just as Hannibal moved it out of his reach.

"On that day, I lost a brother and my sight," Hannibal said with a heavy heart.

"We shall drink together," Scipio offered.

"Perhaps another day," Hannibal said. "Do you know that I have drank more tonight than I have in my entire lifetime? No. I will enjoy the pleasure alone."

Scipio sauntered over to the slain legionnaire and closed the dead man's eyes. He then tore a length of cloth from the man's tunic with his *gladius*. Scipio knelt before Hannibal and tied the fabric around his wound. "You must--"

In gratitude, Hannibal clutched Scipio's forearm. "The bleeding never stops."

Scipio continued to wrap the cut. "I need you alive, my friend."

"To be alive." Hannibal delighted in the thought as Scipio finished making the tourniquet and took his seat.

Scipio folded his arms in disgust. "In many ways, the ghost of Hamilcar lives within you. How could a father ask a son to bear such hatred?" Scipio realized how hypocritical he was at that moment. Did not Scipio the Elder instill within me a lust for war and a hatred of Africans throughout the Mediterranean? he thought. Indeed, Scipio the Younger's passions were no less a consequence of his own warrior upbringing.

Hannibal sipped his wine. "His hatred soon became my own driving force. The death of Hanno ensured that."

Near Chateauqueyras, Alps—218 B.C.

Three months after they departed New Carthage, Hannibal's troops had at last reached the Alps. The climb was steep, and the ice-covered paths were treacherous. At cloud level, the strong winds and the lack of any vegetation were hard on the diverse group of men, except the small party of captured Gaul who had become mercenaries in Hannibal's army. These battle-tested warriors, many of whom were suffering from severe frostbite, were clothed in the animal fur that they had recovered from past vanquished enemy. They also covered themselves in a thick layer of oil for warmth. Fatigue and sickness caused some of the men to stagger as they walked. One of the twenty remaining Indian elephants in the rear guard let out a final cry and keeled over, knocking several Carthaginian and Algerian infantrymen over the ledge and down into the valley floor thousands of feet below. The wails of the doomed beast and warriors echoed through the ranks.

The accident drew the attention of several of the men, including an Iberian soldier who, in the commotion, brushed his pack against a young Gaul named Ducarius. A large man with golden, scruffy hair and an unusually clean-shaven face, Ducarius voiced his displeasure in his Gallic dialect and shoved the Iberian to the ground. The Iberian retaliated by pushing the much taller man backwards. Ducarius unsheathed his iron long sword and readied himself for melee as his fellow Celtiberian warriors cheered for the removal of the Iberian's head. Other soldiers looked on as well, grateful for the momentary diversion from the brutal march. The Iberian unsheathed both his short swords and twirled them in anticipation of combat.

Before they were able to clash, Maharbal approached on his horse and dismounted. The steam shooting from his nostrils announced his deep anger to the men. Forming a "T" shape with his torso and arms, he repelled both combatants backwards. The Iberian was furious, but did not protest. Ducarius, on the other hand, did not back down. Maharbal unsheathed his broadsword and placed the tip of the blade an inch from the Gaul's throat.

"You do not understand Numidian, but do you understand this, Gaul?" Maharbal grinned.

Ducarius stepped away. Maharbal sheathed his sword and remounted his horse as smoothly as he had alighted. Gisgo approached on horseback moments later.

"What happened?" Gisgo searched the men's faces for answers.

"Keep your savages in check, Carthaginian," Maharbal screamed. He then prodded his steed and rode off.

Gisgo watched the cavalry commander leave from the corner of his eye and then focused his rage at the men beneath him. "Secure that elephant for nourishment! We may need it."

Further up the column, Hannibal and Mago rode side by side on their mounts, and the main Numidian cavalry meandered behind them. Mago reached over and placed a hand on the exhausted Hannibal, who nearly fell off his horse in a daze.

"Older Brother?"

Hannibal endured his fatigue and focused on the infantrymen and the rocky path ahead.

"We should have searched for Hanno's body. He should have received the ritual of death," grunted Mago through the heavy beard that now covered his dry lips.

"I know," Hannibal said.

Mago looked on with sympathy. "Your eye."

"Synhus believes that it was the marsh air." Hannibal felt it necessary to quickly put an end to Mago's attempt to console his brother. "Do not worry. I have another."

Mago nodded. "Of course you do." He would expect no other response from Hannibal.

"I remember when Hanno would flee from a butterfly with no wings," Hannibal said. "He became a very strong and brave warrior." His smile disappeared. "This was my war, not his."

Mago managed to contain his rage for a moment. "The war belongs to us all."

Up ahead, one of the Iberian infantrymen collapsed from exhaustion. An Iberian officer rushed over and scolded his compatriot in their native tongue, kicking him to his feet. Hannibal rode ahead of Mago to the scene of the disturbance and dismounted his horse. Hannibal shoved the officer, helped the fallen Iberian to his feet, and hoisted him upon his horse.

"Rest on my steed," Hannibal said.

Hannibal glared at the officer as the other soldiers marveled at his kindhearted gesture. Hannibal then surveyed the men that surrounded him. They were cold and hungry. For some, the trek had already vanquished their spirit.

Hannibal found a high rock to stand on, to get a better view of the thousands that followed him.

"I have lost a brother, and I go on!" Hannibal began, gaining the immediate attention of his men. "The end is near, and Rome is even closer. How can you not go on? The man beside you has gone to battle with you. Regardless of your different beliefs and appearances, you fight together. How can you not go on? Soon you will have riches beyond your wildest dreams. How can you not go on? And when the Romans are surprised when we arrive at the doorsteps of Rome, it is because they did not believe that we could go on." Hannibal smiled to all his men. "As I am plundering their coffers for all the treasure my horse can carry, I will respond, 'How could I not go on, you Roman bastards?'"

The men roared with laughter.

The tone of Hannibal's speech grew somber. "We must go on. We must go on!" He then led the horse with the Iberian slumped over its back by the reins and led his men onward.

The trek through the treacherous mountains had taken its toll on the Carthaginian army, many of whom were wounded, cold, sick and diseased. The oxen trekked along at a crawl. Hannibal sat alone upon his elephant, Surus. His chin rested in his chest, and his hands were loose on the reins of the massive beast. Fatigue and malnutrition showed in his face. As he led the caravan, Hannibal squinted through his undamaged left eye as the glare of the sun bounced off the mounds of snow before him.

Hannibal raised his hand, bringing his troops to an abrupt halt. He stepped down onto the rope ladder and dismounted Surus. Mago, Gisgo, Maharbal, Synhus and the soldiers watched their leader walk forward, gingerly at first and then with more authority once the numbness departed from his legs. Carefully placing his fur-covered boots in the deep snow, he continued on to a place where further egress was impossible. Hannibal stood at the apex of the Alps.

Mago, Gisgo and Maharbal approached Hannibal, awed by what they saw. The officers stood shoulder to shoulder.

"Beyond the Po, there lies Etruria." Hannibal pointed to the misty lands beneath them.

"You were right, General. We have made it to Etruria." Gisgo grinned with sweet sorrow.

"Rome is not far," Maharbal said.

"I never thought it to be possible." Mago's excitement was tempered by his utter exhaustion.

The three officers continued to behold the vast lands beneath them as the infantrymen began to trickle in behind them. They were heartened and proud of what they had accomplished. It had taken five months, and Hannibal knew the cost for his path to vengeance. Disease and skirmishes had diminished the ranks, and he was now left with only forty-five thousand troops. He had lost a brother and half his eyesight. Yet he also knew in his heart that the real battle had not begun. He would have to pay more—much more.

The majestic Roman Senate building was lined with statues of Saturn, Mars and other symbols of the gods. Torches along the Senate floor illuminated its chalky walls for the benefit of the congregation that had gathered there that evening. Scipio the Elder and Scipio the Younger, dressed in their ceremonial armor, were surrounded by the members of Roman Senate, who were seated upon the stadium-style benches of the chamber. In the Grand Chair sat Fabius.

"There is a menace hanging over the empire of Rome. It seems that Hannibal has accomplished what we had thought to be impossible. How shall we prepare to deal with this assault?"

Scipio the Elder stepped forward. "My Lord, I shall move my legions to Liguria. We will crush the Carthaginians before they step one foot into Etruria."

There was grumbling among the graying men of the Senate until Fabius raised his hand to command silence. "I see," Fabius continued with a stoic expression. "The Patriarchs have concluded that Rome would be better served if another consul was elected. Tiberus Sempronius shall therefore support you in your endeavors."

From out of the shadows stepped Tiberus Sempronius, dressed in a fitted tunic. He was tall, young and devilishly handsome—every quality Scipio could possibly despise in an adversary.

Fabius's appointment of Sempronius gnawed at Scipio like mites do an open wound, but he managed to restrain his emotions and refrain from lashing out. "I do not understand, My Lord. Perhaps the new consul should remain in Rome for security measures."

"I have no desire to steal your thunder, Consul, only to repel our African invaders," Sempronius interjected.

"It would be impossible to steal something that far out of reach, Consul," Scipio retorted.

"Sempronius is of equal status, but will provide support by way of Ariminium, should our Carthaginian friend decide to perform a Punic trick." Fabius wanted to defuse the situation before tempers flared between the two Roman officers.

Scipio unsheathed his *gladius*, stepped forward and

placed it on the marble floor before the Senate. Scipio the Younger observed his father with astonishment.

"The African will never enter Etruria alive. Even further, I swear before the Parcae that the only part of Hannibal that will enter Rome shall be his head, right here before you."

Fabius rolled his eyes as a father would to a petulant son. "We are not concerned with your choice of body parts, Consul. Just ensure that he does not slip past you again."

Scipio lifted his chin and put fist to heart. As the consul and his son headed for the exit, Scipio shot a menacing look to Sempronius, who returned it with a deceptive smile.

16.

The Po River and its tributaries split the open plain in several directions. On the north side of the Ticinus Tributary, Scipio the Elder, Scipio the Younger and their legions waited in battle formation with golden standards raised high. Mounted on their stout horses, the tribunes observed the enemy before them. Ahead, on the same side of the river, marched Hannibal's army in ranks of eight across. They marched toward Scipio's army, stopping six hundred yards away. A centurion raced up on horseback to report his findings.

"The Carthaginians appear to number twenty-thousand or so, Consul. Some cavalry, but mainly infantry."

Scipio the Elder raised his hand in acknowledgement, and the centurion rode off to join the ranks.

Scipio the Younger turned to his father. "Perhaps we should await the arrival of Sempronius."

Their aide concurred. "We have not faced this army before, Consul. Prudence would be the best course of action."

Flush with confidence, Scipio ignored the warnings and suggestions of everyone around him. "Neither of you have faced an army such as this, but I have, many times in Sicily. They are nothing more than a band of mercenaries. One display of Roman might, and we shall watch them retreat, as it was with Hamilcar."

"But they have made it this far, Father," the younger Scipio protested.

"Yes, to Etruria. Etruria!" The consul clenched his reins

tightly and gritted his teeth to the point of grinding. "These bastards are threatening our homes, and I am going to push them back into the mountains and let the Gaul sort them out. You do want to defend your home, do you not?"

"Of course, Father," Scipio conceded.

"We will no longer wait for them to make the first move. This time, we shall strike first. Tribune, commit Cohorts One through Five," Consul Scipio ordered.

"By your command." The tribune gave a fist-to-chest salutation and signaled the trumpeter, who sounded his horn five times. The cohorts returned these blasts with a series of short notes. Supported by the cavalry, the legionnaires marched forward, their long, semi-cylindrical shields at their sides.

At their camp further up river, Hannibal, Maharbal and Gisgo observed from the view of their mighty steeds the slowly approaching columns of Roman legionnaires.

"It did not take much to goad Scipio into a fight. He is confident," Hannibal said.

"This was your father's view as well. We have battled him before," Maharbal said.

Gisgo, the consummate strategist, raised an obvious question. "Our heavy infantry is as powerful as theirs, but can we afford the casualties now? There are many."

"Send in the Taurini first."

Maharbal and Gisgo were dumbfounded by Hannibal's order.

"The Gaul slaves?" Maharbal exclaimed.

"Arm them and move them to the first rank," Hannibal replied more forcefully.

Gisgo raised another objection. "General, we are well

aware of their deep disdain for us, but they are a small force. Will they really risk certain slaughter at the hands of the Romans?"

"I believe they will fight. Maharbal, position your cavalry at the flanks. When I give the signal, attack. Do as I command."

Gisgo received his marching orders and darted off. Also, Maharbal rode away, kicking up a trail of dust.

Hannibal galloped up to the confused Gaul slaves who were being herded to the front of the Carthaginian formation. Gisgo and several Iberian officers were tossing swords, shields and spears at their feet—a spectacle that amused the well-oiled soldiers behind them. Hannibal dismounted, unsheathed his sword and addressed the Gaul in their native language, which he had acquired in past battles.

"You men have a choice. Remain as you are, slaves doomed to endure painful, miserable lives that will end in a pitiful death. Or, take up these arms in loyalty to Carthage and be free. The decision is yours." Hannibal stared down the army before him. The Gaul looked to each other for answers as Hannibal turned to address the entire Carthaginian line.

"This choice is for all of you. Look how far we have traveled, over mountains, through rivers, to the battlefield upon which we now stand. There is no turning back. We must now face the ultimate question, conquer or suffer a fate worse than death at the hands of our bitter foes. If we fight with the strength of many nations, all the treasures of Rome shall be ours. As conquers, we shall sip the wine of Rome in honor of those comrades who have given their lives on the battlefield in the service of our noble crusade."

The men cheered. Hannibal turned to the Gaul, who began arming themselves, awaiting Hannibal's orders. The men behind them roared, hoisting their weapons high in the air. Hannibal returned his short sword to his scabbard and circled the formation.

Synhus addressed Hannibal apprehensively. "Will you lead them into battle?"

Hannibal nodded, peering into the eyes of the old mystic. It was the same look he had given him on the roof twenty-years ago—bold yet afraid. Synhus returned Hannibal's nod and reached into a small pouch. Hannibal closed his eyes, and Synhus smeared three red streaks under the blind right one.

"May Ba'al give you the vision to achieve victory," said Synhus.

Hannibal opened his eyes with a look of affection, which transformed into a stern expression of anger and determination.

Battle of Ticinus

Almost five thousand Roman legionnaires marched in tight formation, their sandals rumbling the ground beneath them. Their *scutums* protected most of their bodies, and their bronze helmets glittered in the bright sun, as did the golden-hued armor adorning the thousand-strong contingent of horses in the army's two adjacent cavalries. They were greeted by the barbaric cries of two thousand Gaul, Celts and Iberians running at full-speed.

The clatter of armor and swords meeting shields or other swords pervaded the battlefield. Next heard were the horrific screams of Hannibal's soldiers, who were either being sliced by *gladii* of the enemy or pierced by their *pila*. The Roman cavalry trampled those who dodged the assault and Hannibal's men began their retreat. They were no match for the Roman hastati and principes.

Within the main Roman camp on the outskirts of the raging battle, Scipio the Elder shared a confident smile with his aide. However, Scipio the Younger remained concerned.

"They are easily pushed back," the consul boasted. "Let's squash them all. Send in the entire force."

His aide peered over his shoulder to ensure he understood his commander's order. "The entire force, Consul?"

"I shall lead us to victory, once again." Scipio drew his sword and rode ahead, followed by his son and the tribune.

On horseback ahead of the main army ranks, Hannibal and Gisgo watched the retreat of the Gaul, Celts and Iberians. Thousands of soldiers awaited the arrival of Scipio's heavy infantry as it marched forward with its cavalry on its wings.

"They have committed. Begin the advance forward, but remain in narrow ranks to hide our numbers," Hannibal shouted to Gisgo. "Now dismount! I can't afford to lose my best officer to an assassin's bolt."

Gisgo obeyed his commander's order. Upon reaching the infantry, he alighted from his mare and sent it trotting off. A heavy drum began beating rapidly. Gisgo donned his helmet, raised his shield and twirled his blade above him. "Remain in your ranks! Forward on my command!" His orders were translated into the diverse tongues of the soldiers behind him.

Hannibal now approached the line on his steed. He dismounted, grabbed the javelin and shield from his saddle, and took his position within the ranks.

Maharbal's Numidian cavalry flanked the column of soldiers at each wing. Maharbal inspected his men with a grin. His mare galloped in all directions, warm air jetting

from her nostrils. He dashed over in Hannibal's direction.
"The cavalry is ready."
Hannibal donned his helmet. "See you in the middle."
The Romans were giving full chase to the retreating contingent of Carthaginians, cutting them down as they fled. With their *gladii* and javelins in hand, Consul Scipio and Scipio the Younger led the attack with the cavalries flanking each end of the Roman infantry.
Less than a hundred yards away now, the charging Carthaginian army opened up its ranks. Like an eagle spreading its wings, the Numidian cavalry expanded outward and created a long frontline that was nearly half a mile long.
"More heavy cavalry?" Scipio the Elder muttered.
The twenty thousand Carthaginians and the twelve thousand Romans clashed just north of the tributary. At first, the Romans had a clear advantage with their protective shields and long javelins. The Carthaginian and Iberian soldiers were able to penetrate the Roman army's frontline, and the Celtiberian, Celts, Libyans and Algerians exploited the opening and sliced through the Roman forces.
Outnumbered and outclassed, the Roman cavalries were being crushed by the Numidian troops as the Carthaginian infantry slowly closed in. Scipio soon realized that his army was caught in a chaotic vise and surrounded. The screams of dying Romans penetrated the consul's back and vibrated up his spine.
"Fight, men! Fight in the name of Rome!"
Scipio the Younger fought bravely alongside his father. He planted his javelin into the chest of a charging Carthaginian soldier and then turned his stallion around to slash an Iberian who was attacking the consul. Scipio the Elder could only manage a reckless swing of his *gladius* in

defense.

"It was a trap, Father!"

Not ten feet away from the father and son, Maharbal galloped in on his steed, gutting and dismembering every legionnaire in his path with his broadsword. He commandeered several of his horsemen to search for another point of attack.

A Roman centurion slashed Gisgo across his side. He covered the blood flowing from his wound with his hand, spun around and decapitated his assailant. Gisgo then slumped to the ground in pain. He was fortunate enough to have been discovered by an Iberian soldier, who pulled him out of danger.

Hannibal fought with an uncontrollable rage amidst the slaughter. He launched his spear and repelled a *gladius*-wielding Roman, cutting him down at the knees. His eyes darted from side to side in search of more adversaries.

"Scipio!"

The dust and chaos began to settle. The grassy plain was covered in the red and gold bodies of Roman soldiers, along with a number of wounded or dead Carthaginians. Consul Scipio was wounded in a sword attack. He hobbled around in a semi-conscious state, supported by his son, as the wails of the fallen Romans soldiers reverberated across the battlefield. Exhausted and out of breath, Scipio the Younger swung his *gladius*, in an attempt to protect his father from the enclosing enemy soldiers.

"Back, savages!" The young man steadied his sword and hunched over for balance.

A Celtiberian soldier lurched forward with his sword drawn. "We're going to slice you in half, Roman swine."

Scipio the Younger swung once more, but the weight of

the blade and his extreme fatigue nearly toppled him. He regained his balance but not before the Celtiberian was able to slice his arm, causing Scipio to drop his *gladius*, along with his now unconscious father. Scipio fought the urge to screech in pain.

"Stop!"

The soldiers turned around. Hannibal and Maharbal were riding up on horseback. Both men wore the scars of battle. Hannibal dismounted and drew his sword. "Their commander belongs to me."

Hannibal approached Scipio the Younger in catlike fashion. He extended the tip of his blade to within inches of the Roman's throat. Scipio pulled a small dagger from his belt and held it up in a pathetic bid to defend himself. A crazed, frightened look then overtook the young man's face as he stood between Hannibal and his father. Scipio the Younger could hardly stand. Tears rolled down his cheeks.

"Kill him! Kill him!" The chant arose from the mercenaries in Hannibal's army. The plea grew louder as the infantrymen joined in and demanded Scipio's speedy death. Hannibal observed the sporadic pounding of Scipio's chest, and soon his thirst for blood softened into a feeling of empathy. He lowered his sword and sheathed it. The chant from the soldiers ceased.

Hannibal mounted his horse and bent down to address the two powerless Roman leaders. He spoke in refined Latin. "I spare you for only one reason. Tell your Roman Senate to leave my city before I arrive. My generosity stops here. Submit, and Rome will not burn. Continue to challenge me, and every man and woman in Rome will be crucified in the name of Ba'al." Hannibal turned to an Iberian officer. "Ensure them safe passage, along with ten of their legionnaires."

The officer nodded. Hannibal gave Scipio the Younger a final look from above and galloped off. Maharbal followed. They negotiated their horses through the thousands of dead and wounded men. Carthaginian medics tended to the wounded. In the distance, raging Celts and Gaul were taking hundreds of Roman soldiers prisoner.

"Why did you not kill them?" Maharbal asked.

"All in good time. For now, they are necessary."

Maharbal shook his head in disapproval. "A dead man seeks no vengeance."

"I understand," Hannibal said.

"The men may see it as weakness."

"Do you see it as weakness, Maharbal?"

"Your father would have never done such a thing. But you may be smarter than Hamilcar ever was. What do we do with the prisoners?"

"Keep as many as we can as slaves," said Hannibal. "The others, what do I care? Kill them. That should expunge any suspicions about my weakness as a leader."

"Gisgo!" The sight of Gisgo being cared for by Synhus stunned Hannibal. Gisgo lay against a fallen horse and Synhus was applying an herb and bandage to his wound. Hannibal dismounted and raced over to them.

"I am okay, General." Gisgo's grins were checked by periodic grimaces of pain.

"Ba'al was with you," Synhus interjected.

"I will be ready."

Hannibal smiled and placed a sympathetic hand on Gisgo. He looked toward the Po River on the horizon.

"Be ready, Mago. More is sure to come."

17.

Sempronius's legions had arrived. The men had repast and settled in for the night in anticipation of the next morning's battle. Wounded Roman legionnaires continued to hobble into the camp, which was situated near a tributary of the Trebbia River and patrolled by several Roman sentries.

In his command tent, Tiberus Sempronius sat comfortably in his tunic, petting a rottweiler that sat at his feet and staring across the table at a tired and bandaged Scipio the Younger.

"I will pray to Mars that your father recovers fully," Sempronius said.

"He is badly injured," Scipio replied, bowing humbly. "We are fortunate to be alive. Before we knew it, we were surrounded...I mean...We never had a chance. Father is awake now and doing better."

"Good. It is a shame, however, that he did not wait for my arrival. With only a half-day's march, we could have turned the tides, and he might have been celebrating instead. I do wonder why the Punic spared your lives. Any thoughts?"

"Their leader, Hannibal, gave us safe passage." Scipio worked his way to the edge of his seat. "I am not sure why. Perhaps to toy with us."

Sempronius took a deep breath. "I see." Sempronius stood and poured himself a goblet of wine. Gesturing, he offered Scipio a drink. Scipio declined with a shake of his head. Sempronius commenced sipping.

"He let us escape for a reason," Scipio said.

"Escape?" Sempronius chuckled. "He slaughtered most

of your legion."

"We were just the bait. He is waiting for you. If you are planning to strike blindly, he may have already anticipated your move. We should return to Rome and fortify--"

Sempronius smashed the goblet on the ground. "You wish to rob me of my glory?"

"No, I am simply--"

"You are young. You do not understand the strategies of war. I have over forty thousand men at my command. From the intelligence you have gathered, that is a two-to-one advantage."

"This man, Hannibal, he does not see advantages," protested Scipio. "He finds a weakness and he exploits it. Your men have marched many miles. They are without proper rest."

"My men are of no concern to you!" Sempronius's patience had worn thin and Scipio knew that the man was beyond reasoning.

"I mean no disrespect to you, Consul," Scipio said calmly. "But before we even had a chance to fight, we were defeated."

Sempronius studied the map on the table.

"I must admit, the strategy that the Carthaginian implemented was well done, but I like to think that the better consul is prepared for their tricks."

"Fool," Scipio mumbled.

"You have something to say, Tribune?"

"Only that I pray that your keen leadership guides us to victory."

Scipio's deferential remark appeased Sempronius's ego. "Perhaps I shall give my legions the rest they need and attack in a fortnight. You are very astute."

"Thank you, Sir."

Heavy galloping and shouting outside the tent interrupted their conversation. The two men darted out of the tent to determine the source of the disturbance.

Sempronius was astounded and enraged by the sight of more than two hundred Numidian horsemen throwing flaming javelins through the cold air and into the snow-covered Roman camp. Wave after wave of Numidian horsemen launched their projectiles and galloped out of the reach of their victims before they could retaliate. Several javelins ignited Roman tents while others landed in the bodies of Roman men. Their *gladii* drawn, the Roman soldiers scattered amidst the chaos. Several of them gave chase as the Numidians rode off.

"The nerve of that bastard!" Sempronius selected a passing legionnaire and clinched his collar, pulling and pushing to release his rage. "How dare he hide under the cover of darkness!?"

"It is a trick," Scipio said.

"I do not care! At dawn, I will do away with this Carthaginian swine once and for all."

Scipio moved to within inches of the consul's face. "You must not do that!"

Sempronius released the soldier in his grasp and proceeded to wag his index finger at Scipio. "I must not? Just watch me."

Scipio's resigned himself to the finality of Sempronius's decision as several Roman officers accompanied the commander to his tent.

At nightfall, Hannibal's tent was illuminated only by the soft glow of the moon. His eyes closed, Hannibal sat cross-legged, praying before a statue of Ba'al. He remembered the promise that he made to Hamilcar, the drawing that Hasdrubal had given him and the smile of Hanno. Sweat trickled down his bald head as he lost himself in deep thought.

Hannibal opened his eyes.

The long column of over forty thousand Roman infantry and cavalry marched eight abreast across the Trebbia River, whose steep banks were covered with heavy brush. On horseback, in the middle of the column, were Sempronius and Scipio. To complement his cocky persona, Sempronius had donned a helmet with an eighteen-inch crimson plume, which made him resemble a vibrant peacock.

"A beautiful day for crushing a foe," he shouted.

Scipio scanned the terrain but saw only the dense, thorny brush surrounding the Trebbia.

Battle of Trebbia

Just over thirty thousand Carthaginian soldiers stood ready for battle on the snow-covered plain. The infantry was in the middle of the formation, flanked on both sides by cavalry and elephants.

Hannibal sat atop his steed and observed Sempronius's army a few hundred yards away. He donned his helmet as Gisgo approached. Gisgo was still anguishing from his earlier wound. He labored his way to Hannibal, his bandage protruding from his corselet.

"You cannot take me out of this fight!" Gisgo said.

"Gisgo, you are wounded. I cannot afford to lose you this

early in the campaign."

"I am ready."

"You cannot even mount a horse. You would serve me better in the command tent."

Gisgo lowered his head. "I am sorry, Hannibal."

"Give yourself time to heal before the next battle, which is sure to come," Hannibal said.

Gisgo nodded in agreement and walked away. Hannibal scanned his army in search of Ducarius.

"Ducarius!"

The Gallic warrior stepped out of his place in the formation and obeyed Hannibal's summons. Hannibal honored the soldier by speaking to him in his native language. "You shall lead the infantry into battle."

The fur-clad, pale giant flashed a half-smile and resumed his haughty posture. "Thank you, General."

"You will fight with the fierceness of a lion, and you will then fall back in retreat," Hannibal said sternly.

Ducarius was dumbfounded. "I do not understand."

"Nor would I expect you to, my Gallic friend, but do it nonetheless."

Ducarius nodded and returned to the ranks. Hannibal turned to Maharbal, who was mounted with his Numidian cavalry. Hannibal greeted him with an assertive closed fist. Maharbal returned the salute and secured the reins on his steed. As was the case at the dawn of every battle, Hannibal observed Synhus praying in the distance, his warm breath streaming into the cold air.

The Carthaginian and Roman infantries clashed just east of the river. The cries from both armies were accompanied by officers shouting orders and encouragement. The two sides appeared to be equally matched at first, but soon the Gaul infantry led by Ducarius began a slow retreat.

On one flank of the Carthaginian infantry, elephants trampled some of the enemy hastati, but the aggressive Roman cavalry were able to repel the massive beasts. Led by the battle cries of Maharbal, the large contingent of Numidian horsemen once again engaged their Roman counterparts. As the two cavalries exchanged iron sword and javelin blows, men on both sides fell.

Sempronius and Scipio observed the contest as the main infantry stood ready to move forward. A quaestor, or lieutenant to the consul, steadied Sempronius's horse.

"Ah, we are winning," Sempronius said with confidence. "It is to the swift that victory belongs, Tribune."

"It is my opinion, Consul, that the soldiers should have been properly fed and rested before we faced the Carthaginians," Scipio said with the strongest of convictions. He knew all to well what ill-prepared leaders could do to the souls of men.

"There you are again questioning my leadership. Enough!" Sempronius's tirades often surfaced like flashes of insanity unleashed from deep within him. "Whether you accept it or not, Mars is with Rome not with these savages." Sempronius pointed to the battlefield. "Observe! My strategy is working to perfection. We are winning! I have the best triarii in the Roman army. I shall lead the main force personally and claim complete victory in my honor."

"Consul?"

Before the young Scipio could protest further, Sempronius unsheathed his *gladius* and hoisted it into the air.

"Onward!"

The trumpets commanding the formation worked their way through the lines, and soon the main Roman force was marching toward the frontline. Sempronius and Scipio trotted along on horseback.

The middle ranks of the Carthaginian light infantry collapsed and Sempronius had now committed his main forces to the battle. Taking stock of these developments, Hannibal waved his heavy infantry forward. They shook the snow-covered ground as they moved in quickstep to engage the Romans. Hannibal charged ahead on his steed. The Carthaginian heavy cavalry was met by fleeing Gaul and Iberian light infantry. Many fell to their deaths before reaching safety. The advancing Roman velites and hastati pushed forward. Their weapons clashed. The forces were well matched at first. Although the Romans had driven the elephants away, the Numidians were soon able to overpower the enemy cavalry. Their spears gored the Romans and separated them from their horses. Maharbal had the sneer of a madman as he hacked his way through the lightly armored Roman velites.

Sempronius and Scipio soon found themselves in the thick of the battle, slashing downwards at the Carthaginian infantry from their mounts.

"The cavalry is broken, Consul!" Scipio had been nearly ousted from his horse by an Algerian spear. "We must retreat before it is too late!"

Hannibal had dismounted his horse and was swinging his sword through the mayhem. He sliced below a Roman soldier's scutum, splitting his legs below the knee. Hannibal spun around to evade another adversary's *gladius* and deftly removed the man's throat. Because his blind right eye had left him with reduced peripheral vision, Hannibal was slow in responding to a charging Roman's scutum. He was knocked to the ground by the power of the shield. The soldier pounced on Hannibal, ready to deliver a deathblow with his *gladius*. He was thwarted, however, by Hannibal, who with his lightening-quick reflexes was able to roll out of the way in the nick of time. The Roman soldier continued to strike as Hannibal defended himself from his disadvantaged position on the ground. The Roman soon had the best of Hannibal and disarmed him of his sword. Fatigued, Hannibal awaited his fate. But just as he was about to strike, the Roman was gutted from the back by a long sword. Behind him was Ducarius with eyes wide open and drool spilling from the corners of his mouth. He nodded to Hannibal with a smile as the Roman slid down his blade. Hannibal leapt to his feet and returned Ducarius's nod.

"Now, Mago," Hannibal whispered.

At the point where Sempronius had crossed the Trebbia River earlier, the deep banks with their heavy brush revealed their secret. From within the foliage emerged one thousand Carthaginian infantry and one thousand Carthaginian horsemen, standing in unison. Mago commanded the band of mercenaries and wasted no time in implementing Hannibal's strategy. He unsheathed his sword.

"Attack!"

The remaining Roman infantry was falling back as the Carthaginian cavalry engulfed them. Nonetheless, the Romans fought on bravely. Sempronius and Scipio were now on the defensive, fending off the surrounding Carthaginian army. Scipio held on tight to the reins of his horse to avoid falling off.

"Fall back, Consul!"

"Yes, fall back!" the panicked Sempronius agreed.

As the Roman soldiers began their slow retreat, Sempronius spun around just in time to see Mago and his unit charging toward them from fifty-yards away. His jaw fell to his chest.

"Pluto's wrath," he whispered.

The retreating Romans were surrounded and cut to pieces. The screams of the dying men served only to further instill fear in the fleeing soldiers. The few stragglers who were able to fight their way out sought refuge in the cold waters of the Trebbia. Those who were slow on foot were hacked to bits by the pursuing Carthaginian, Iberian and Gallic infantry before they could reach safety. The Numidian cavalry also chased down the few remaining Roman horsemen. Sempronius was on the verge of crying as Scipio grabbed the reins of his horse and used his *gladius* to forge a path through the surrounding Carthaginians.

It was a massacre.

The field of snow was now covered with bodies and blood. The Roman soldiers were straggling across the Trebbia, but many were gouged in the back by Gallic long swords as soon as they entered the water, which was already full of floating corpses.

Hannibal looked on, wiping the blood from his brow as the men cheered the name of their general. "Hannibal! Hannibal! Hannibal!" Hannibal gazed at the battlefield, the carnage and the stench death. His eyes closed, and he was transported to a familiar dreamscape.

The nine-year-old Hannibal struggled to hold his breath. He managed to grab on to something to prevent himself from sinking deeper into the river of blood. To save himself from drowning, Hannibal attempted to hoist himself up on the object floating next to him. Hannibal, in horror, realized that this object was the body of Hanno, floating dead in the river with his eyes open. Not Hanno the man, but Hanno the child. He was bloated and his skin was rotten. Hannibal pushed off and propelled himself to the surface. He coughed and cried as he attempted to breathe.

18.

Bithynia, Asia Minor—182 B.C.

Hannibal opened his eyes. He leaned over and would have fell out of his chair if not for Scipio supporting the aged Carthaginian's shoulders. Hannibal pushed him away with the hand that was not clutching his wound.

"Get away from me, Roman!"

Scipio was surprised by Hannibal's response. "I was simply trying to help you."

"Scipio Africanus," Hannibal said with a coy grin. "You do not look African." Hannibal chortled uncontrollably.

"I am not amused." Scipio began with a serious look but soon joined Hannibal in uncomfortable laughter. As their mirth faded, Scipio sat once more.

Hannibal took another sip of wine. "This wine was made from the best vineyards in Apulia. I have saved it all of these years."

"Another symbol of your rape of my country," Scipio said.

Hannibal slammed his fist on the table and several items crashed to the floor.

"You say that to a man who spared your life?"

"You spared nothing! Nothing!" Scipio reined in his emotions before continuing. "You allowed my father to live so you wouldn't discourage Sempronius. For if a consul had died, the other consul must await the election of another consul before he could engage in battle. Your espionage was very good."

"What does Scipio's life have to do with yours? Perhaps you were spared because I understand what it means for a son to lose his father in battle. You have much to learn about men."

Scipio believed that Hannibal was being sincere.

"But if I had known then that your father had connived my father's death, I would have crucified him and returned him to Rome in pieces."

They stared intensely into each other's eyes.

"I have no doubt of that," Scipio said.

Carthage, Africa—217 B.C.

A lone Carthaginian guard's heavy footsteps echoed in the cold, hollow chamber. He approached the men of the Suffete seated high behind their podiums. He handed Senator Bragibas a scroll and left the room. Bragibas untied the parchment and unfurled it. After taking a moment to review the document to his satisfaction, Bragibas passed it to the next man.

"General Hannibal has reached the Po and is moving into Etruria." Bragibas was relieved by the news.

There were murmurs of joy from the other senators. One was especially astonished. "Ba'al. And General Hannibal has accomplished this even though all of his elephants were lost in a winter storm upon arrival," the senator marveled. "There shall be a feast created for him upon his arrival in Carthage!"declared another. Soon the entire chamber resounded with words of praise for Hannibal's achievement. The body was silenced, however, when the letter reached

Senator Cobo, who received it with a cynical smirk.

"We now have the Romans by their throats." Cobo's mouth watered with insurmountable greed. "I must admit, I never thought the boy would get this far."

"The journey must have taken its toll on his resources," Senator Bragibas said. "We must send reinforcements. We will enact a new tax to supply the war effort."

"No. Let us see what transpires."

"What?" Bragibas could not comprehend the logic of Senator Cobo.

"I suggest we send a delegation to Rome to negotiate for peace."

Bragibas was alarmed that the other senators were nodding in agreement with Cobo's proposal. "What makes you think that peace is in the best interest of Carthage?"

"We will undoubtably receive better terms than Hamilcar. But we must act now," Senator Cobo said with confidence.

Bragibas rose from his senatorial throne. "Perhaps we will win. Perhaps with support from the Suffete, we could have Rome and all of Latium. Let General Barca finish what he has begun."

"You have more faith in this boy than you have in all of Ba'al's Kingdom," Cobo chuckled, entreating the other members of The Hundred to join him.

Yet Bragibas stood strong. "Yes I do." As an officer in the first Roman War, his convictions were highly honored by his men.

"As you had with Hamilcar?" Cobo retorted.

An uncomfortable silence prevailed. Bragibas gathered himself and gritted his teeth. The sparring began once again. Bragibas thought of the days of old when he would have snapped Cobo's head from his diminutive frame. He often took solace in knowing that it was still possible.

"Senators, this is not the time for impetuous thinking. Do you not understand the ramifications of attacking Rome while a peace treaty is in effect? The only thing they will negotiate for is our crucifixion before the Roman populace."

A younger senator stroked his beard and concurred. "Hannibal has come this far. I agree with Bragibas. The spoils have been generous."

Cobo leaned over to sneer at the senator, who recoiled from Cobo's sharp stare. "This Hannibal leads a ragtag group of bloodthirsty mercenaries, and you wish to drain our coffers in support of him. May I remind you that it was not long ago that such men turned on Carthage? But nonetheless, we shall have a vote, Bragibas."

Each man in the chamber reached down and set two small, brilliantly colored stones—one a majestic shade of violet, the other a dim emerald—on the podium before him. The stones glittered in the light that beamed down from the torches overhead.

Bragibas stood. "I propose the creation of a tax to go before the Assembly in support of the efforts of General Hannibal Barca in Etruria." He nudged his violet stone to the edge of the podium.

Now Cobo stood. "I propose the creation of a delegation to negotiate a peace with the Romans...with the Suffete in complete control of the operation, of course." Cobo pushed forward his emerald stone with a single finger.

Each senator contemplated his vote. Some even glanced over to Cobo, seeking his approval. One by one, the men began to nudge their emerald stones to the edge of their podiums.

Angered by Cobo's grin, Bragibas clenched his stones.

He could not win in the face of political corruption.

Located within Campus Martius of Rome stood the beautiful Temple of Mars. It was adorned with majestic stone statues of the Roman god dressed in full battle armor, including his crested helmet and sacred Ancile shield. In the center of the temple stood the largest sculpture, which depicted Mars in his chariot, lance in hand. Scipio the Younger knelt in the dimly lit chamber, praying before the sacrificial altar.

Out of darkness, Fabius entered the sanctuary in his toga.

"Should you not be at the Temple of Pluto, begging him not to accept your father?"

Scipio completed his prayer and stood to face Fabius. "I asked Mars to guide Father in his next battle with the Carthaginians."

"Next battle?" Fabius said, intrigued.

"Surely, Father will recover and Sempronius--"

"Has been replaced," interrupted Fabius. "And your father will not recover soon enough." Fabius walked over to the altar and whisked his hand through the fountain filled with the purified water. "The people of Rome are in a panic. They believe that this Hannibal will kill them and steal their children in the night. And why would they not, five legions decimated in a matter of days."

"Who have they elected?" Scipio said.

"Flaminius and Servilius have been elected new consuls."

"And what of Father?" Scipio felt the disgrace that his father was sure to face after losing the office of consul to a plebian.

Fabius could feel the grief emanating from the young tribune. "Once your father is healed, the Senate will have use for him and yourself. You have made quite a name for yourself, Young Scipio. Sempronius holds you personally responsible for his survival."

"And now he is humiliated as a failure." Scipio donned his cape, enveloping his tunic. Scipio bowed to his superior and proceeded to exit the place of divinity.

"I will pray for your father," Fabius said to the retreating Scipio.

Scipio paused. "Thank you." He then departed, leaving the future dictator to contemplate a solution to the Carthaginian storm slowly approaching the Italian countryside.

Hannibal's army was camped along the Po River. Snow covered the frozen plain, and the sound of the water trickling across the stones in the river was muted by heavy, celebratory drumbeats.

Hannibal, his officers and the Insubres Gaul tribal chief—a rather muscular middle-aged warrior with long, graying hair and a stern face—were being entertained by a group of half-naked Insubres women, performing their traditional dance. The shadows created by the moonlight and the raging fires were hypnotic. Seated between Hannibal and the chief was the sub-chief, a very powerful-looking man, whose fur and gold adornments suggested that he was of a higher status than even the chief. On the other side of Hannibal were Maharbal, Gisgo, Mago and Synhus, who were all drinking heavily. All around the campsite thousands of soldiers drank, danced and fought occasionally for the rights of a woman.

The chief mumbled in his native tongue as he continued to admire the dancers. The sub-chief translated for Hannibal. "He says that he knew you were coming. Chief says he has heard of you from the other villages. He wonders how a man can lead so many yet not enjoy the pleasures of libation."

"Tell him that Rome shall be my libation," Hannibal said sternly.

The sub-chief translated Hannibal's reply. Seconds later the chief laughed for all to hear.

"He says try not to drink it all at once. He would also like a taste."

"The Romans possess many lands."

The sub-chief translated and the chief nodded in approval. The chief continued to speak in his deep, gritty voice, and the sub-chief once again conveyed his comments. "He is indebted to you for driving out the Taurini. The warriors that you request will be supplied."

Hannibal smiled and thanked the chief in the Insubres language. "I am humbled. Your generosity is appreciated."

In a drunken stupor, Mago leaped up and mocked the dancers by dancing himself. "It is such a beautiful existence! The dark skies above are only the beginning."

Maharbal laughed. "You are speaking nonsense, and you cannot dance. Please, cease your foolishness!"

"I dance like a Numidian hyena." Mago waved his arm before the Numidian horseman, taunting him.

"Yes, and you battle like one, too!"

The venerable Synhus wrapped himself tightly in his ceremonial robe and uttered departing words into the cold, misty air. "I will retire now, General."

"Yes, my friend, take your rest." Hannibal gazed upon Synhus with warm eyes. Hannibal was worried about the health of the aging medicine man. Furthermore, Hannibal depended on Synhus for guidance and reason as had Hamilcar. He wanted to leave Synhus under the protection of

Hasdrubal, but he knew that the old man would refuse due to the oath he pledged to Hamilcar so many years ago.

As Synhus was preparing to retreat into the darkness, Mago attempted to block his departure with his comical antics. "Synhus, where are you going? The celebration has just begun." Synhus ignored him and continued on.

"Perhaps it is time you rested too, Brother." The truth was that Hannibal felt responsible for the behavior of his officers. Hamilcar had taught him to hold all those who served under Ba'al accountable. However, Hannibal expected such behavior from one of his foreign mercenary soldiers not from his brother, a son of Hamilcar Barca.

Mago twirled around in bliss and almost stumbled over the seated Hannibal. "In the last several months, I have almost frozen, starved and been killed. I think it is comprehensible to find sanctuary in the flask, do you not?"

As Mago twirled away, Hannibal snarled at his brother. "You are an officer from Carthage, behave like one."

Mago ceased his dance. "Behave? Behave? Just who do you think you are criticizing, Brother? You forget, I am of your same blood. Just because you sit here and do not savor libation or enjoy the pleasures of women does not allow you to order me to behave!"

"You are embarrassing yourself." Maharbal had enough as well.

"Stay out of this, Numidian!"

The celebration around them continued, although the Insubres chief now focused on the conversation between the two Carthaginians. He leaned over to his sub-chief and beckoned him to translate.

"You think that just because Father chose you to go to Hispania that you are better than me, superior to me?" Mago shouted.

Gisgo walked over to assist Mago. "You are tired like all of us, Brother."

Mago shoved him away. "Get off me! You are no brother of mine. I have only two brothers. I used to have three until we followed the dreams of the Chosen One and his dead father."

Rage began to flicker in Hannibal's eyes. He stood and approached Mago. Those in the immediate area looked on with uneasy anticipation as the drumbeat continued. Mago returned the gaze of the approaching Hannibal with equal intensity. Hannibal, without hesitation, backhanded Mago, causing him to stumble.

"You have had too much wine, Brother." Hannibal watched Mago regain his balance. The drumbeat ceased, and the surprised soldiers and officers looked on.

Mago's eyes watered from his pain and anger. He reached for the hilt of his sword, ready to unsheathe it. Hannibal was disappointed and dismayed that Mago would be foolish enough to draw his weapon on his own brother. But Hannibal did not flinch. He stared at Mago, almost scolding him with his gaze. Mago could no longer face Hannibal. He lowered his head and then spat on the ground. He wiped the bloodstained grit from his lip as Hannibal shook his head and walked away into the darkness, addressing the chief with a slight bow on the way.

Away from the celebration, Hannibal retrieved his cloak to stave off the brutal icy winds that were drifting in from the mighty Po. The ivory moon reflecting off the snakelike tributary was the only source of light in the starry night.

"Hanno."

Hannibal fell to his knees, and tears began to stream

down his face. He allowed himself a few seconds to let out his emotions before swiveling his head around in search of any witnesses. In the distance, he heard the crackle of a wild beast's claws upon the dry snow. Hannibal unsheathed his short sword and maintained a defensive posture. His eyes darted to locate the origin of the camp intrusion.

Across the riverbank, Hannibal could see the lion that had so often haunted his dreams—or perhaps it was an illusion. Regardless, a chill ran through his limbs as though he had fallen into the water. The lion observed Hannibal and then cantered away in the opposite direction. Hannibal sprinted to the edge of the bank, but he had already lost sight of the beast.

Battle of Lake Trasimene

Only faint images of the still body of water peeked through the heavy morning fog that covered Lake Trasimene and the foot of the Cortona Mountains nestled beside it. The passage between the foothills and the lake proved to be narrow for Flaminius's legions. The mile-long column was forced to march four men abreast along the damp, muddy, three-mile path.

Flaminius, pompous and handsome in a feminine sort of way, trotted his way on horseback through the cautious Roman soldiers and made his way toward the front of the line. The cavalry followed him. He squinted in search of the enemy through the hazy mist.

"I cannot see anything in this fog. But the Carthaginians cannot be far," Flaminius remarked to the tribune beside him.

Once at the head of the column, Flaminius could make out Carthaginian banners that were held aloft by columns of marching soldiers. "There! There they are! We've got them from the rear. We shall lead the charge. Advance Cohorts Eight and Nine for the final blow."

"By your command, Consul. Cohorts Eight and Nine, advance!" The tribune commanded the trumpets to drive the men into a faster pace. A thick, impenetrable mist enveloped the path, forcing each legionnaire to rely on the man before him for guidance.

Flaminius removed his *gladius* from its scabbard and kicked his steed to into a faster trot. Horsemen followed behind him with *pila* ready to launch. The supporting velites and the triarii, armed with their *hastas*, or thrusting spears, began to pick up the pace in anticipation of battle.

The fog cleared ahead for Flaminius, and he was left breathless by the sight. What he thought was the rear guard of the Carthaginian army was only a couple hundred men facing him, swords drawn.

"A Punic trick!" bellowed the horrified Flaminius. He was indeed correct.

From the side of the Roman column, spears darted out of the mist and found their targets in the Roman soldiers' chests and necks. Soon Carthaginian army foot soldiers sounded their frightening battle cries. The infantrymen and Numidian horsemen attacked the Roman flank from out of the fog-covered mountain and cut the Roman soldiers down before they could react. The Roman legion was in a panic.

Mago, Gisgo and Maharbal were also in the thick of the fighting. Hannibal led the charge, displaying his ferocity with every swing of his sword. "Cut the Romans down where they stand!"

Flaminius watched in horror at the chaos behind him. His

men were retreating in all directions, hoping to avoid meeting their doom at the end of a spear. Some attempted to flee into the water but were run down by the Gaul, Africans and Iberians. Many drowned after being impaled in the back by Numidian javelins. Flaminius shrieked in anger and charged the wall of Hannibal's men on his mount, swinging his *gladius* in desperation. A few Roman horsemen who accompanied him were dragged from their horses, slashed and dismembered. Somehow, Flaminius managed to maintain his mount—and his confidence. "Men, fight to the death! Reward their trickery with a sharp blade."

But before Flaminius could continue with his one-man crusade, a javelin pierced straight through his abdomen. He fell to the muddy earth and faced the man who had ended his life. Ducarius stood over Flaminius with a cold expression. The blood of his other opponents covered his pale face.

"That is for laying waste to my village." Ducarius brought his sword down on the doomed consul and lifted his head to the sky as his personal trophy.

Hannibal surveyed the destruction of the Roman legion and the dead afloat the waters of Lake Trasimene. More blood had soaked the earth, and he was once again victorious. Hannibal removed his bronze helmet and let it fall to the ground as his men began to pilfer the Roman dead in celebration.

19.

Bithynia, Asia Minor—182 B.C.

Hannibal had a look of satisfaction.

"I had all of Etruria before me, ready to be taken."

Scipio smiled and reached for Hannibal's carafe of wine. Hannibal pushed it casually out of Scipio's reach.

"That wine is Apulian. Therefore, it belongs to the Roman people and me," Scipio said.

"This is not for you."

"It soothes my impatience, which is growing as we wait here. I must return you to Rome before you very well bleed to death."

"I doubt I shall bleed to death. Though it would be a fitting end to a bloody past, the pain, the screams, the stench of thousands dead before your feet." Hannibal could see his past as well as he could feel it. "There is something else we share, Consul."

"What would that be?"

"Redemption."

There was an eerie silence in the room.

"After Lake Trasimene, your people elected Fabius, the dictator."

"The Cunctator."

"The coward," Hannibal interjected. "But it mattered not."

Central Campania—217 B.C.

The golden sunset created a heavenly glow around the lengthy peak of Mount Massicus. The foothills at the base were covered with Roman legionnaires preparing for camp. Serfs began cooking the evening meal as the men set up their tents.

As one would expect of a shrewd man, Fabius's tent was a dreary accommodation with nothing more than a cot, table and a few personal items. Marcus Minucius, a fiery and handsome young Roman officer with auburn hair, returned the fist-to-chest salutes given by the Roman guards outside Fabius's open tent. He darted past them, removed his bronze helmet and entered to see Fabius standing over a map on a table, dressed in tunic and chainmail corselet. Minucius placed his fist over his heart and raised his palm to Fabius. "Sir?"

Fabius studied the map with chin in hand. He waved the young officer closer to the table. Minucius approached with the pride that came from being a dictator's second-in-command.

"We have Hannibal's army trapped," Fabius said without taking his eyes off the map. "Our garrison at Beneventum guards the east, the Volturnus protects the south and our cohorts at Cales provide a suitable barrier to the west. Needless to say, I would rather be in Rome."

"Yes, My Lord. It appears we have him." Minucius smiled profusely.

"As my Master of the Horse, what strategy would you recommend?"

Fabius's inquiry struck Minucius as sincere. Minucius took a moment to study the map and pointed with his index finger. "The Carthaginians only escape route is through the northern passes. If we send Cohorts Ten and Seven into the hills to draw them out, we can set up an ambush along these paths, crushing them before they know what has hit them."

Fabius nodded in approval. "Interesting."

"Thank you, Sir."

Fabius eyed the officer. "You were born in these lands, correct?"

"Yes."

In fact, Minucius was the first *cives sine suffragio* to reach the rank of Master of the Horse, sole lieutenant to an elected dictator. Fabius knew that this was due to his non-Roman family's patriarchal connections.

"A very beautiful place," Fabius added.

"I am proud of my home." Still, the young lieutenant wondered where the dictator was taking such a conversation.

"Very good." Fabius focused his attention on Minucius. "Your knowledge of the terrain will be useful, which is why I chose you to accompany me."

"I am honored," Minucius said with a slight bow.

Fabius resumed studying the map. "Your strategy is lacking, however."

"Sir?"

"So far, this Hannibal has destroyed countless legions." Fabius directed Minucius to the map below. "At Ticinus and Trebbia, we lost over thirty thousand men. At Trasimene, I lost a consul and fifteen thousand men and cavalry. They suffered only fifteen hundred dead. And every scouting party I sent was either wiped out or captured." Fabius's thin brows rose to meet his thinning hairline. "It seems that every battle ends with a Punic victory. How would another attack be any different?"

Minucius considered for a moment the angles of attack. "We will use the terrain to our advantage. The men are rested and eager for battle."

"I suggest that the best way to defeat an army that obliterates you in every battle is not to battle them at all."

"Sir?"

"Attacking would be foolish." Fabius's tone of voice conveyed a hint of disappointment with Minucius's military strategy. "We will continue to monitor the enemy and win the war of attrition."

"But we have them trapped!" The young, inexperienced officer showed his impatience.

Fabius eyed Minucius once more with a stern expression. "Master of the Horse, under no circumstances are you to engage the Carthaginians. Do I make myself clear?" Fabius rarely showed emotions to anyone. But when he did, they were sincere and unbending.

Contribute it to his overzealousness, but Minucius felt obligated to question any order that appeared detrimental to the overall end result. However, Fabius was not a consul to dispute. The Senate elected him Dictator. Still, as Master of the Horse, he deemed Fabius's tactics as weak and harmful to Rome.

Minucius raised his voice. "I disagree with--"

"Thank you, Marcus. Await my next orders."

Fabius returned to the map, ending his consultation with Minucius, whose mouth was open, ready to protest. Fabius turned to him with a decided fierceness. For in his military training, a warrior must first learn obedience.

"You are dismissed."

Minucius refrained from further debate and donned his helmet. He saluted and departed the tent as Fabius resumed studying the map.

Days had passed with no engagement. To calm his blood, Minucius toured the region. Followed by several centurions on horseback, he stopped at the edge of a bluff overlooking the vast and fertile fields of the Falernian Plain. The lush flora was in full bloom, decorating the panoramic landscape with their vivid colors. Tiny villas were scattered across the plain. With a hardy smile, Minucius protected his eyes from the glare of the sun.

"Lentulus, over there, just past that ridge is where I came of age," Minucius said.

A thin, twenty-year-old centurion named Gneaus Lentulus scanned the region. Minucius and the inexperienced soldier entered the Roman army at the same time and trained together in Tarentum, located in southern Apulia.

"It is beautiful, Commander," Lentulus said.

"Yes, it is. And when this is all over, I plan to return here to marry and have many children."

"Very good, Commander."

Minucius's subtle smile was erased immediately. The other officers also took note of what had caught his attention. "I do not believe it."

Galloping along the Falernian Plain was Hannibal, followed by eight of his Numidian horsemen. They stopped and formed a line in the tall grass, directly facing Minucius's small party.

"They must have traveled from the hills." Lentulus was thrilled with the sight of the Carthaginian. "Is that him? Is that Hannibal?"

"Perhaps." Minucius squinted for a clearer view. "I believe so." He leaned back, sporting a devilish grin. "Of course, who can really tell them apart?"

The officers laughed.

"But what are they doing?" Minucius said.

Lentulus drew his sword. "Commander, shall we ride down and attack. We outnumber them."

"As much as I welcome your suggestion, Lord Maximus warned me of such Punic tricks. This could be one of them."

Hannibal and the horsemen raised torches simultaneously from their sides. A flame was lit and passed among the men. Even from the distance that separated the warring parties, Minucius could see the maniacal glare in Hannibal's eyes, a look of satisfaction and provocation.

Lentulus leaned in further. "Sol will not set for hours. Why...?"

Suddenly, Minucius's mouth dropped in horror. "In the name of Mars..."

Hannibal and his men lowered their torches, instantly igniting the dry field below them. Several of the Numidians also splashed oil from huge vases, causing the flames to spread even faster. Hannibal gazed into the eyes of the Master of the Horse.

"No!" Minucius could only cry out in despair. His beloved homeland up in flames. Minucius pulled at the reins of his steed and attempted to ride past the centurions. Lentulus was able to grab a piece of the enraged man before he sped away.

"No, Commander! It could be a Punic trick, remember?"

Minucius fought to break free, but Lentulus held on, assisted by the other centurions.

"Those bastards! How could they do such a thing?" Minucius was reduced to pitiful tears.

"Commander, we must report this to the consul!"

Lentulus shook Minucius in an attempt to draw him out of his uncontrollable rage. Minucius struggled a little longer before succumbing to reason. He pushed the men away and gritted his teeth in frustration.

Hannibal trotted off with his men.

Later that night, the smoke from the earlier fires still darkened the sky. Campfires illuminated the Roman encampment as the men prepared to retire for the evening. However, before they could do so Lentulus burst into the camp, flush with excitement. He had overheard Minucius giving orders to his officers for the night and reported his findings.

"Commander, the Carthaginians are moving!"

"Moving?"

Lentulus ran off and Minucius followed. They reached the edge of the camp and Lentulus pointed to the dark mountains above. The men could see hundreds of torchlights marching in single file up Mount Massicus.

Minucius's eyes sparkled with excitement. He tapped his comrade on his breastplate. "They think they can escape under the cover of darkness, do they?"

"Shall we investigate, Commander?"

"Yes. Send a messenger to the consul. Devious bastards."

"By your command." Lentulus sprinted off.

The trumpets sounded reveille to alert the camp. A combination of Roman soldiers and cavalry were soon advancing on the parade of torchlights traveling up Mount Massicus. Minucius was ahead of the pack with *gladius* drawn.

Fabius was preparing for sleep when a Roman guard

entered his tent unannounced. "Consul!"

Fabius was startled for a moment and stopped what he was doing. "What is it, sentry?"

"The Carthaginians are moving up Massicus!"

"At night?"

"Yes, Consul. The Commander has taken a sizeable force to intercept."

"He did what?"

The guard gave a quick bow and darted out of the tent.

Minucius was within a hundred feet of the torchlights and waved his cohort onward. "Full attack, men!"

The war cries of the Romans were fierce.

Elsewhere in the hills surrounding Massicus, Hannibal and his army were marching through the thick-wooded path along the embankments. Hannibal swayed back and forth in his saddle, accompanied by Gisgo, Synhus and Mago on their steeds as well.

"When one cannot find a way, he makes one," Hannibal said.

Gisgo enjoyed the confidence of his young commander. "We should be clear before they discover your strategy, General."

"Very clear, Gisgo."

The cohorts and Minucius charged at the torchlights with weapons drawn. Within moments, they discovered that the torchlights were not carried by Hannibal's men but were tied to the bridles of cattle, which bellowed in excitement at the approaching Romans. Minucius had been outsmarted and it showed on his face. The Romans lowered their weapons, looking to their leader dumbfounded.

"A Punic trick," whispered Minucius.

Utterly surprised, Minucius and his men were attacked by a flurry of spears zipping through the air. The silhouettes of a small force of Numidian horsemen revealed themselves to the Romans. The spears found their mark, piercing the unsuspecting Romans' skin. The battle cries of the Numidians were haunting and dispiriting. Minucius watched as his men fell one after the other, unable to collect themselves and defend against the invisible enemy.

He turned to Lentulus. "Full retreat! We must alert the legions!"

Before the centurion could obey his order, a spear caught the officer in the back and knocked him from his horse. The dark warrior Maharbal grinned with satisfaction.

"Lentulus?" Minucius watched his friend take his last breath.

Eventually, increasing numbers of Numidian horsemen enclosed the retreating Romans, and many of the legionnaires were cut down before they could escape. Wielding his *gladius*, Minucius battled for his life.

Several cohorts accompanied Fabius on horseback to the site of the Numidians' ambush. The bodies of Roman legionnaires were scattered along the hillside, Numidian spears protruding from the torsos of many. The moans from those barely alive did not faze the stern Fabius. He gritted his teeth and surveyed the dead. Two field medics were dispatched to attend to the wounded Minucius. He was stunned, and his armor was covered in blood. "The Numidians...they were just waiting for us."

As he passed Fabius, Minucius gazed at his general who

babbled his way into unconsciousness. Fabius waved the litter-bearers away, and they hurried off with Minucius. Fabius was left to ponder the ramifications of Minucius's impatience.

20.

Cannae—216 B.C.

Helmet in hand, Hannibal stood in full armor on the eastern bank of the shallow Ofanto River. The glow from the sunrise gave him a beautiful aura. He wore a light beard now, which aged him slightly. Hannibal's eyes were concentrated on the Roman encampment across from the Ofanto River, just outside the city-state of Cannae. Before him ninety thousand Roman soldiers were amassing. Mago, also in full battle-dress, approached.

"There are so many," Hannibal confided in his brother.

"Yes, there are, Brother," Mago said with bravado.

"A true test for the Lion's Brood."

Mago turned to Hannibal. "You said that once before...the Lion's Brood."

"Father never spoke many words to me. So at night I would sneak away to listen by his chambers as he drank with his officers. That was his name for us, his Lion's Brood. It was very hard for him to show his love, but he was very proud of us, Mago."

"The Lion's Brood." Mago paused for a moment, and the words seemed to give him a sense of contentment.

"Remember the day before I left with Father?" Hannibal said.

"Yes." Mago remembered it well. It was the day that they left their childhood behind.

"Would you have jumped?"

Mago had not anticipated Hannibal's question regarding that so many years ago. He was taken aback for a moment, but he soon visualized the bluff near their home in Carthage. "Yes," Mago responded.

Hannibal nodded with a smile. "When I left Carthage, I carried with me all of my brothers." Hannibal faced Mago. "That is the part of you I took with me."

"What part would that be?"

"Your fire."

Mago smirked and continued gazing down at the river below.

"I carried Hanno's strength and purity. I carried Hasdrubal's defiance. But without your fire, your strength of heart, I would have perished long before today." Hannibal placed his hand firmly on Mago's shoulder. "Any of you could have become what I have become and led so many to destiny. If you were chosen, you would have taken parts of us with you because that is the bond we have. You must know that."

Mago could not utter a word. It was all he could do to fight back his tears. Just as Hannibal searched for approval from Hamilcar, Mago sought it from Hannibal, his older brother. He was bitter about having been left alone with their mother and brothers. Who did he have to emulate and depend on? Hamilcar robbed him of Hannibal, and for that, he hated his father. A tear escaped from his eye, and Mago wiped it away before it reached his cheek. He turned to Hannibal and grasped the hand Hannibal had placed on his shoulder.

"I grow weary, Brother," Hannibal said. "But I realize that if we fail, our children and their children will suffer. Father knew it, and I know it now."

"It is a heavy responsibility to bear," Mago said.

"Yes, but I do this for Giscon."

Battle of Cannae

The massive armies of Carthage and Rome faced each other across the vast plain, just east of the Ofanto River. Their banners snapped in the wind.

The Roman velites stretched almost a mile across, supported in the rear by the hastati and principes with the Roman and Etruscan cavalries on the flanks. Their four generals were on horseback, ahead of their respective legions. Consul C. Terentius Varro, an experienced soldier with a hawkish face and intense eyes, commanded the Etruscan cavalry. Consul L. Aemilius Paullus, a large, paunchy man, commanded the Roman cavalry. Proconsul Gnaeus Servilius, a veteran warrior with a rugged, whiskered face commanded the infantry in the middle, along with Proconsul M. Atilius Regulus, a clean-shaven and statuesque young officer.

Hannibal's ragtag army numbered only fifty thousand. Hannibal surveyed the enemy from his steed. Balearic slingers and pikemen were positioned at the front and center of the force. Iberian and Gallic light infantry, commanded by Hannibal and Mago, were behind them. They were flanked on both sides by the heavily armored African infantry, lead by Gisgo. Maharbal commanded the Numidians on the farthest right flank, while Sosylos, a battle-tested Iberian officer, headed up the Gallic and Iberian cavalries on the left.

"They outnumber us almost two to one!" Gisgo shook his head in amazement as he saw the vast legions of Romans before him.

Hannibal nodded. "Yes they do, Gisgo! But for all their

numbers, they are still missing something most essential to victory!"

"And what would that be, General?"

"I do not see one Gisgo in their ranks!"

Gisgo laughed and galloped off.

Hannibal turned to face his men, his horse restless, dancing and neighing to the wind. "Men, do you hear me?!" The men cheered. "In three great battles, we have routed our enemy, decisively! I have delivered all that I have promised. You have gold! You have savored victory! Today, I have no more words. Today is a day reserved only for fighting! If we are victorious today, Rome belongs to us! And you will know wealth beyond your wildest dreams! Yes, today the words cease, and we shall fight! Today, we shall prove that Rome belongs to us!"

The men cheered and banged their weapons, eager for battle. Hannibal and Mago dismounted and took their places in front of the infantry. The drums sounded, signaling the start of battle.

The slingers began marching in a quickstep and were met by a phalanx of Roman velites. The slingers launched their stones of death. Some of the projectiles bounced off the enemy's shields while others connected with Roman heads. Soon both armies collided in a full sprint. Carthaginian pikes pierced Roman torsos while the velites cut down the bare-chested slingers. The velites overwhelmed the Balearics by their sheer numbers. The survivors began to fall back to the Carthaginian lines.

Twirling his *gladius* in full gallop, Varro waved his entire army forward. The trumpet sounded.

As the Balearians beat their hasty and pitiful retreat, Hannibal ordered his cavalry onward. His forces were soon raining bloody strikes upon the heads of the Roman legions. Maharbal alone cut down several Etruscan horsemen. Their horses danced around each other as each man tried to maneuver for a clean strike. The Numidian long spears found their marks. Sosylos hacked his way through the Roman infantry with his broadsword. He came face to face with Aemilius and exchanged iron blows.

The main Roman hastati and principes marched in tight formation toward the Gallic and Iberian infantries. Hannibal raised his fist, and the foreign line formed a semicircle, the center moving forward while the side remained stationary. Once they found their places, the Gaul and Iberians lowered their spears and followed a charging Hannibal and Mago toward the approaching Roman infantry. Seconds later, the two forces clashed. The Romans continued to march forward as the Carthaginians penetrated the Roman lines. Their armor clashed against the tall Roman shields. The Carthaginian army's battle cries mixed with the wails of fallen men. *Gladii* met spears, and the blood flowed freely as the savagery of the battle escalated. The combatants slayed each other without mercy, clawing and biting like wild animals.

Hannibal impaled a legionnaire with his sword. He twirled around and used his shield to throw a Roman soldier off balance before cutting him down at the waist.

Mago swung two swords, slashing and jabbing. Half his armor covered from the blood of others.

The Gaul and Iberians were retreating as the Romans appeared to be overpowering Hannibal's men. From their steeds, Servilius and Atilius drove their men forward.

"Fall back!" Hannibal ordered.

Hannibal and his men withdrew to their original line of defense and held their ground. The Gaul and Iberians inverted their semicircle formation, formed a wall and collapsed its ends on the Romans. The drumbeats became heavier, and the two flanking African infantries, led by Gisgo, constructed a jackknife around the Roman legionnaires, who soon found themselves surrounded. The fierce Africans began to overpower the fatigued and confused Roman soldiers.

"They are attacking our flanks!" Atilius shrieked.

"Fight on, men! We have them!" Servilius would not surrender.

Atilius peered over his right shoulder and was aghast by the sight the Iberian and Gaul cavalry bearing down on a flank of Roman soldiers, who were in total disarray. He then looked over his left shoulder and saw Varro's cavalry being cut down as they fled the battle. To his rear, he could hear the battle cries of the Numidian horsemen.

Atilius threw his helmet to the ground for clearer vision. "Servilius, signal a retreat!"

Servilius swung wildly at the swarming Carthaginians, fighting for his life. "There is nowhere to--"

Before he could finish his sentence, a javelin whistled through the air and pierced his armor through the back. He fell from his horse and was subjected to the repeated thrusts of African swords.

"Mars, save me!" Atilius was lost.

Maharbal darted past the proconsul and launched a javelin through his back. He screamed in agony before falling to the corpse-strewn battleground. Maharbal circled around Atilius and dislodged his javelin from the mortally wounded man.

As Hannibal slew one of the last-standing Roman combatants with his *gladius*, he was caught off guard by the grip of a man's hand on his shoulder.

Mago stood before him, armor splattered with blood, rocking back and forth. Mago removed his helmet, which tumbled forward as his body collapsed to the ground. Hannibal rushed to Mago's side, his attention riveted on his brother's deep, labored breathing and the large, gaping wound in his midsection. He was oblivious to the boisterous sounds of his men, who had begun celebrating their victory.

"Mago!" Hannibal caressed his brother's head in his lap and tried to lift him up. "Mago, no. No! No!" Hannibal wiped the blood rushing out of Mago's mouth.

"Brother?" Mago's eyelids fluttered, and his irises shifted from side to side.

"Mago, do not die. You are alive!"

Maharbal rode up and dismounted. He knelt on Mago's other side. Synhus approached.

Mago clenched the tunic sleeve underneath Hannibal's corselet. "I do not want to die here, Brother."

"Synhus, help him!"

Synhus looked at the wound. "Hannibal, I cannot help him. He belongs to Ba'al."

Hannibal lifted his sword to within inches of Synhus's throat. "You save him, or by Ba'al you will follow."

"Hannibal!" Maharbal grabbed the blade with his large hand and lowered it to the ground.

"Synhus, help him!" Hannibal cried.

"Take me home, Brother." Mago struggled to breathe as tears flowed down his cheeks.

"Breathe slowly, Brother." Hannibal rocked Mago, trying to console him.

"Hanno and Hasdrubal...Hannibal." Mago smiled. "Take me home."

"We will go home together." Hannibal returned his smile.

Mago held on tighter. "Brother?"

"I am here, Brother."

"I do not want to die, Brother. Not here..." Mago's bloody frame trembled and convulsed. As he stared into Hannibal's eyes, his body went limp, and he took his last breath.

Hannibal cried out, his shrieks reverberating throughout the surrounding forest and across the vast skies. Tears trickled down his dust-covered cheeks as he closed his brother's eyes. Maharbal and Synhus lowered their heads and each placed a single palm upon Mago's chest.

Maharbal stood. "We will ride the winds. If we leave now, we can soon have Rome by its throat. We shall have our revenge!" Hannibal did not hear him. Maharbal shouted in his deep, gritty voice. "Hannibal?!"

Hannibal held his brother in his arms, rocking him.

"Hannibal!" Maharbal tried once more.

"Forgive me. Forgive me," Hannibal whispered into Mago's ear with eyes closed.

Maharbal turned to Gisgo, who approached from the rear. "He knows how to conquer but does not know how to use it. Truly, your god has not bestowed all things upon the same person." With that, Maharbal stormed away.

Hannibal surveyed the mounds of dead, the wounded pleading for death, the Roman soldiers who had buried their heads in the earth. As the tears rolled down Hannibal's face, his eyes told of the horrific realization to which had just came to past. He held his brother tighter. Gisgo saw his mighty general crumbling before his eyes, and he too was reduced to tears.

Bithynia, Asia Minor—182 B.C.

Hannibal grimaced, squeezing the bandage on his wound. "I knew what it meant to battle...to kill...to die. Yet I always thought that I could protect them."

"I sympathize." Scipio looked on with all sincerity.

Hannibal gazed straight ahead with sunken eyes. "My son. Whatever occurs today, promise me that my wife and son will not be harmed."

To Scipio, those sounded like the words of a dying man, and it concerned him. He made sure that Hannibal's bandage was secure and that the bleeding was under control.

"That I promise."

21.

Saguntum, Spain—214 B.C.

"Giscon, be careful!" Imilce snatched her four-year-old son just before the boulders shattered against the outer protective stonewall of the spire, rumbling the dark staircase leading to safety. Imilce lost her footing but was able to avoid tumbling to sure injury or death. She gripped the torch tightly with one hand and Giscon with the other as they made their way down into the subterranean caverns. She remembered Hannibal's description of these caves and how the governor had designed them to reach the harbor. They maneuvered through several Iberian warriors rushing headlong in the opposite direction with bows and swords in hand. Native Iberian screams meshed with the sounds of explosions and metal clashing upon the walls of the fortified city.

Saguntum was under attack. The Roman armies and siege engines, led by the importunate Publius Cornelius Scipio the Elder and his brother Gnaeus Scipio, surrounded the fortified city. Wave after wave of Roman maniples, heavily armored hastati, and lightly equipped leves ascended the wall—only to be repelled back by determined Balearic slingers mounted atop the wall. The unfortunate legionnaires not climbing the assault ladders were drenched in scalding oil and set afire by Iberian archers in the towers. Yet Scipio the Elder would not be denied his triumph. He pressed on, sacrificing many of his men. His perseverance would bring its rewards. After three months of continuous attack, countless fiery salvos, the wall was shredded and legionnaires battled with Carthaginian mercenaries in the streets of Saguntum. The flames rising from the wooden structures exemplified the Romans were gaining the upper hand in the battle.

Surrounded by his loyal tribunes, Scipio the Elder watched the assault from the comfort of his horse in the rear echelon command post. His hair was stark white, thin as feathers and flailing in the wind. His face drooped with folds from his eyes to his chin. Even the injured, limp arm he sustained at the Battle of Ticinus did not deter this bitter man from entering the battlefield. Scipio wanted revenge for the pain and embarrassment of his defeat near the Po River. He visited his vengeance upon the people of Saguntum mercilessly. No one was to be spared. To Scipio, they were all supporters of Carthage.

A cavalryman approached, quickly dismounted and raised his palm in a salute that acknowledged Scipio's status as proconsul and co-commander of Roman legions in Hispania.

"What is your report?" Scipio said without diverting his eyes from the battle.

The young man was covered with dirt and his face was scarred, though his smile poked through. "The cohorts commanded by Proconsul Scipio have penetrated their resistance, and the commander guarantees that we shall meet within its center!"

"Attack from the north, surprise from the south. So my brother has also had a taste of victory," Scipio said, almost chuckling to the soldiers that surrounded him.

"Pardon me, Sir?"

"Never mind. Inform my brother that I look forward to meeting at the center."

"By your commanded." The soldier mounted his horse and rode away.

"I want this Hasdrubal's head on the tip of a blade. Indeed, any blood of this Punic, Barca, will suffice. Any officer who satisfies my wishes shall be rewarded with land and riches," Scipio shouted.

His tribunes were ready to oblige. Their eyes twinkled at the prospect of receiving such prizes. Each man galloped away on their mounts toward the heart of the melee. Trumpets roared as a subtle smirk animated Scipio's face.

Giscon's weight strained Imilce's trembling limbs, slowing her trek as she carried her son through the dark halls of the dungeon. She did not know where to flee. It was a labyrinth of cobwebbed corners and moldy floors. Wounded soldiers returning from the fighting passed, taking their final steps before falling to their doom. The echo of men and women screaming their last words vibrated through the caverns and coursed through Imilce's diminutive Greek frame. Frantic, she withheld her true fears from Giscon.

"I'm afraid, Mother," Giscon said in his soft, high-pitched voice.

Imilce lowered him to the ground and knelt down to catch her breath. Her ivory dress was now soiled from the muck that trickled down from the rattling ceiling. She gazed into Giscon's bronze opal-shaped face and searched for soothing words to console him. For a moment, she found herself drifting back into the past, wondering about her beloved Hannibal. Giscon looked very much like his father: his eyes, his nose, his Barca brow. She smiled and held tightly to the lad's tunic.

"Do not be afraid, Giscon," Imilce said in Greek. "We

will soon leave from here and return to the land of your father's birth."

"Will I see Father?" Giscon grinned with anticipation.

Imilce wiped her face. "Yes. He is waiting for us there." She knew that she might have very well lied to Giscon. She had not received a message from Hannibal for some time, three years to be exact. However, prior to departing for Africa to recruit new soldiers to defend New Carthage from the Romans, Hasdrubal had reassured her of Hannibal's safety. Hasdrubal could have never assumed that after he left, two massive Roman armies would march on Saguntum and lay siege to the port city. Unlike New Carthage, it did not appear to be the obvious target. Imilce and Giscon were sent to Saguntum on that assumption. Now the city was falling and its inhabitants were at Rome's spiteful mercy.

The rumbling coming down the hall startled Imilce, but she soon realized that the heavy footsteps approaching were a contingent of ten Celtiberian and Iberian infantrymen and a Carthaginian sub-commander. The sub-commander quickly sheathed his short sword and extended a hand.

"Lady Barca, we have searched all of Ba'al's Kingdom for you," shouted the officer over the booming blasts of catapults finding their marks. "We are to escort you to the seaport, where a vessel will take you and the young lord to Tunis."

"Tunis?" Imilce said as she lifted Giscon from the cold ground.

The officer extended both hands and offered to carry Giscon for Imilce. "Commander Barca had a contingency plan in the event of such an occurrence. His sister, Lady Salammbo, will meet you there. But, we must hurry."

Imilce handed her son over to the Carthaginian. The party

then began to flee through the tunnels. Imilce stayed close to the officer and her son. The hardened warriors moved cautiously as though expecting a confrontation. Imilce inhaled the salty smell of sea air and knew that the exit to the dungeon was growing closer. As they reached a fork in the caverns, one straight ahead and another to the right, they discovered that their way out would be contested. Roman leves and hastati filled the tunnel ahead and were fast approaching with their pila and gladii drawn. The Celtiberian and Iberian soldiers stood ready to defend themselves. The officer checked his rear, only to see that there were legionnaires advancing their direction. The garrison had collapsed and only the cunning would escape alive.

"Take that path. Hurry!" The sub-commander handed Giscon to his mother and directed Imilce to the tunnel on the right.

Imilce lifted her son, who was confused at what was transpiring. Her eyes met the fear in his. She knew that the men understood that their chance of survival was slim. They would fight so that she and the heir to the Barca dynasty could escape unscathed.

"Go!" He drew his sword and prepared for the rigors of close combat.

Imilce's concern was keeping Giscon safe. She ran just as the clashing of iron weapons sounded behind her. There were no lit torches in the cavern, only a beam of natural light from an unknown source. The screams of the melee soon dissipated and the patter of her sandals could be heard. Imilce's strength was drained, and she was forced to set Giscon down. Nonetheless, they continued running. Her lungs burned from exhaustion and the dust. They both coughed their way closer to the end of the tunnel, a dead end.

A brick wall barred their way to freedom. The source of the light that helped guide them was a small crack where the foundation of the wall had been shaken. The space was extremely tight but wide enough to tempt Imilce with the idea of shoving Giscon through. Leaning down to get a glimpse of what lay on the other side, she saw grass leading to the waters of the nearby Mediterranean. She leaped up and moved Giscon toward the crevice.

"Giscon, you squeeze through there first, understand?"

Giscon nodded and dropped to his knees. The agile lad snaked his way through the opening, his shoulders giving him the most trouble. With only a few scrapes, he made it through.

"Mother!" Giscon whined.

"I am coming." Imilce lowered herself down and placed her head through the opening. She saw the anxious Giscon holding on to her long, black hair, now sullied from dirt and sweat. Repeatedly, Imilce contorted her slender frame to fit through, but it was impossible. The space was too narrow. Giscon wept as he watched his mother's head disappear from view. Imilce reversed herself and stood in the tunnel, breathing heavily, searching for an alternative. That was when she heard heavy footsteps closing in from the darkness ahead. She had no intentions of finding out if they were friendly or not. With all her strength, she kicked the wall, hoping to free the brick loose or at least widen the opening. But to no avail. Imilce clawed at the mortar until her fingertips became gnawed and bloody. She was trapped.

Imilce fell to the floor and reached through the crack. Giscon grabbed her hand and Imilce saw the anguish in the boy's face. "It is too small for me, Giscon. You must run. I will take another path and meet you by the sea. Understand?"

"No! Mother!" Giscon lay there, holding tight to his

mother's grip. Tears poured down his face.

"My dear Giscon, I will be fine. Understand?" She spoke in a calm tone to reassure her son. "Now do as I say."

"No!" There are times when children cannot discern the complexities of a situation, but they do have the uncanny ability to know when something is wrong. Giscon could not break free of the bond shared between mother and child. He was afraid that he might never see his mother again.

"I will be there soon." Tears welled up in her eyes, but she had to hold them back, for Giscon's sake. Imilce held his two small hands as her jaw fluttered from the agony. "Now hurry!"

Giscon released his hold and crawled backward slowly, wiping his tears along the way.

"Go!" Imilce commanded.

As Giscon obeyed her and sprinted out of view, Imilce gave her heart a moment to remember her son before facing what might come. She jumped up to face the approaching footsteps. The legionnaires helmets glittered in the thin beam of sunlight that penetrated into the cavern. Five soldiers approached, licking their lips at the spoils of their victory. It was forbidden for Roman soldiers to participate in pilfering, rape or lawless murder. However, in a dark, dirty and damp hidden tunnel, such laws were not necessarily applicable. Imilce leaned against the wall and trembled, clutching her shoulder. Somehow, through her crying, she managed to hum. It was the melody that she hummed often, the one that drew Hannibal to her in the past. Perhaps Hannibal will hear me again and come to me once more, she thought. She hummed deeper and deeper as the soldiers moved closer, growing stronger within. One of the grubby men unsheathed his gladius and launched himself at Imilce. But Imilce did not scream. She unveiled a dagger that she had hidden in the folds of her garments and plunged its blade into her would-be assailant's throat. She gritted her teeth and yanked the knife out. The blood of the choking Roman splattered her white dress. She watched him fall with his eyes bulging forward. Quickly, she traded her dagger for the gladius in his scabbard.

"She has the blood of Vulcan running through her veins," shouted another legionnaire as they closed in on her with their weapons drawn.

Imilce screamed and swung wildly at the men. The well-trained soldiers dodged her attacks and repelled her swings. One of the men forearmed her in the face with his bracer. She fell to the floor, dazed and on the edge of unconsciousness. The four soldiers smiled as they turned her over to examine their cornered quarry.

Iberus River, Spain—Winter 212 B.C.

Rome now had a foothold in Hispania. As Hannibal wreaked havoc in central Campania, Roman forces swept through central Iberia. The Scipio brothers took advantage of Hasdrubal Barca's absence and hampered another Hasdrubal, a commander appointed by Hasdrubal Barca to defend Hispania from the Roman legions. He was inept and unable to rally the men to offer a fierce resistance. He fell back to New Carthage. With ease, the Scipios' legions stormed the villages that supported the Carthaginians and made them pay. Valencia, a neighboring settlement of Saguntum, was burned to the ground, and its inhabitants were sold into slavery. Saguntum itself received a more favorable punishment since its citizens did resist Hannibal's invasion six years ago. It was through the intervention of the gods that all of Hispania did not fall into Roman hands. Scipio the Elder became ill and often issued baffling orders to his officers. But Gnaeus Scipio protected his brother and never reported his senility to the Senate.

Scipio the Younger had just been assigned to his father's legion and arrived at his father's encampment only a few days after the massive battles at Valencia and Saguntum. Anticipating that Hasdrubal would soon return from Africa with fresh troops, elephants and zeal to avenge Saguntum, Scipio the Elder had ordered the deployment of extra forces to that city. This proved to be an enormous tactical blunder. It allowed Hasdrubal Barca to take the Roman legions by surprise at Valencia, close in on their rearguard, surround their position, and wait them out. Outnumbered and isolated, the Romans were forced to battle their way to freedom. They were able to carve a path through the Carthaginian line and escape northward to the icy Iberus, but not without cost.

"Father!" Scipio pushed his way through the numerous healers milling about his father's command tent. He let his helmet fall to the ground and took a knee next to his father's cot.

Scipio the Elder lay unclothed, with only a loincloth draped over his abdomen. The wounds that dotted his midsection had been cleansed and covered with peppermint leaves and bandages. Just as a healer placed a blanket on him for warmth, Scipio the Elder coughed up blood-filled saliva. A young tribune grabbed his hand to console him while the healer quickly wiped the spillage from his mouth with a damp cloth. Scipio the Younger snatched the cloth and motioned to the man dressed in the ivory tunic to leave him and his father alone in the airy tent. His father was pale and frailer than Scipio remembered.

"Father, it is I, Scipio."

The dying man's eyes slowly opened and found Scipio sitting beside him. "Son?"

"Yes, it is I," Scipio the Younger said with enthusiasm. Warm steam billowed from his nostrils into the cold air.

Attempting to speak, Scipio the Elder once again spat blood. "The Punics are deceptive..."

"Rest, Father. You are not well." Scipio continued to wipe his father's chin and brow.

Scipio the Elder faced his son. "What of Gnaeus?"

"He is with the gods."

The elderly man whimpered from the news. His obstinacy to surrender his command was responsible for the loss of his brother. He had not felt such heartache since the plague that stole his wife, the mother of his son. He could find consolation only in the knowledge that he would soon see her and his brother before long. His eyes widened and he clenched his son's leather breastplate tightly. "Lake Avernus also awaits my arrival."

"Stand strong, Father," said Scipio as he held his father's arm.

The proconsul's arm went limp and air ceased to pump through his lungs. Scipio witnessed his father's spirit depart the material plane. He folded the arms of the slain general upon his chest and with a wave of his hand closed his eyes. Scipio allowed a single tear fall and wiped it away from his clean-shaven face, ensuring that no one saw him in his moment of weakness. His father was gone. Now he alone sat atop the House of Scipii. It was a heavy burden for a warrior in his mid-twenties to endure. Still, Scipio was now an experienced officer and was tougher and stronger than his soft demeanor suggested.

"Publius!"

Scipio turned around and recognized the legionnaire standing at the entrance of the tent. "Laelius, it is good to see you." Laelius was his childhood friend who had commanded the navy under Scipio the Elder. They had not seen each other since performing their rites of passage in the caves of Samnium. Laelius's hair was cropped all around, and his light beard made him look much older than Scipio. As Laelius approached his comrade, the two men raised their palms to each other.

"Greetings, old friend," Laelius said softly.

"Greetings."

Laelius gazed at the body of Scipio the Elder. "I came to pay my respects before time drew near." Laelius placed a hand upon Scipio's shoulder. "I see that the hour has arrived. I shall offer a thousand prayers to the gods for your esteemed father."

"I would ask nothing less from my dear friend," Scipio said with a subtle smile.

"What will you do now?"

Scipio broke away from their embrace and stated, "I shall take command of my father's legions."

"Publius, that is a decision for the Assembly. It may be viewed as *perduellio*."

Scipio covered his father's face with the blanket. "It was my father who raised these legions, and now they are mine to inherit. Besides, it is only treason if I fail. Will you assist me?"

"Of course."

"I will first see to my father's death ritual," announced

Scipio, "and then I will track and kill this Hasdrubal, followed by Hannibal Barca."

Laelius gritted his teeth and refrained from speaking the truth. He knew firsthand the ramifications of leadership based on revenge. It led to many deaths.

"It is not an act of vengeance, my friend." Scipio faced Laelius and continued. "As a citizen and an officer of Rome, it is my duty to protect her by the means I deem reasonable and best. I have studied this Hannibal thoroughly and know how to defeat him."

"Publius," interjected Laelius sternly, "many men before you have proclaimed that they have studied his ways but have failed."

"That is true. But unlike my predecessors, I have studied him with admiration."

22.

Rome—210 B.C.

A grizzled Fabius peered out the window of his tower overlooking the Roman streets. The people below were in a panic. Mothers were gathering their children, and stores were closing shop in the market area. Soldiers ran to their posts. One merchant tipped over his wagon in an effort to flee.

Six years had passed, and Hannibal continued to unleash his rage on Campania and Apulia. He carried out his rampage of destruction from village to village, though many settlements willingly submitted to the conquering Carthaginians—Arpi, Bruttium and Lucania to name a few. In the meantime, Fabius pursued his counter-offensive strategy: delay any direct engagement and scorch the earth, leaving Hannibal with no resources to feed his army. Yet as the warring went on, Fabius began to wonder whether his actions were in fact prolonging the suffering. He doubted that Rome had the fortitude to last much longer under such conditions. And he was correct. Rome's economy was steadily collapsing under the burden of having to fund the never-ending succession of legions that fell to Hannibal's blade.

Fabius' worries did not end there. Phillip of Macedon also supported Carthaginian interests by attacking provinces loyal to Rome on the Italian coast. Hannibal had even marched on Rome from Capua two years before, only to toss a javelin over the wall. Thus, the panic that was ignited following the slaughter at Cannae grew. Nonetheless, Fabius could not fathom Hannibal's decision not to attack the walls of Rome. Yes, he was well aware that the Carthaginians wanted to create fear in the hearts of the Roman consuls and divert them from recapturing strongholds in Campania. However, he also knew that he had to continue the fight for the future of Rome. Fabius understood that Hannibal was growing weaker with each passing moment. In addition, his strategy favored his legions and not the Carthaginians. "Why does Hannibal continue to hover over us like a horrible nightmare? My nightmare." He contemplated this as a manservant entered the room.

"Lord, Aedile Cornelius Scipio has arrived," said the servant.

"Send him in," Fabius responded without facing him, gazing out of his portal.

"By your command." The servant departed as Fabius closed the window's wooden panels. It was clear that the war had taken its toll on him. He shook as he walked, and his face revealed new lines and crevices. The warrior had grown weaker, but his mind remained sharp and methodical.

Scipio's breastplate rattled, announcing his arrival. The war had also affected Scipio's appearance in a more positive way. A handsome, chiseled face and slender yet muscular frame had displaced his once boyish features. Scipio swung his cape and bowed before the dictator. "By your command."

Fabius faced Scipio, his hands tented before him. "Rise."

Scipio stood.

"Rome will surely be attacked soon. Our tactics have failed and Vulcan has unleashed Hannibal in retribution. We have come to the triarii." Fabius was drawn to a beam of light that had penetrated a crack in the portal. "Over half of our legions have been decimated, and the people are preparing for the onslaught. If we fight Hannibal, we shall lose. If we do not fight him, all of Rome will fall. And we are running out of consuls."

"You brought me from Hispania for a reason," Scipio said.

"Your victories are well noted. Your capture of New Carthage was very impressive. We have a strong foothold in Hispania again due to your legions undoubtedly. I am sorry that your father did not fair as well."

Scipio clenched his lips, took a deep breath and smiled. "He fought bravely."

Fabius paced the chamber. "My religious duties have confined me to Rome, but you have studied Hannibal's tactics, have you not?"

"Yes, I have."

"Go on."

"A man with nothing to lose has every reason to win. He fights without remorse or hesitation...a potent enemy."

"Potent indeed," Fabius concurred.

"For years, Hannibal has pillaged Etruria, Campania and Apulia without any repercussions. Let's take the battle to him. He has a brother in Hispania. We have battled him many times. He is not nearly the leader that Hannibal is. If we could somehow force Hannibal to fight in two places, divide him, we have a chance to save Rome."

"Interesting, but he does not easily fall for trickery."

"There is no trickery. We shall not fight Hannibal directly. We will fight around him. Let us confront the things that matter to him."

"Good...very good. You will sit well as consul, Scipio the Younger."

"I wish only to save our precious Rome because we have indeed come to the triarii."

Canusium, Apulia—208 B.C.

The spacious building was the remnants of what was once a beautiful home belonging to a wealthy Apulian. It had been stripped to the bone, leaving its cold stone walls to flicker in the torchlight. Hannibal sat slumped in his chair at the head of a long wooden table, along with Maharbal, Gisgo, Synhus, Sosylos and Ducarius. A large map of Campania covered most of the table.

"What of Carthalo?" Hannibal said.

"He was unsuccessful, Commander," Sosylos replied.

Hannibal dropped his head. "So there will not be peace, after all."

Maharbal slammed his fist upon the table. "There is no peace! They refuse to negotiate because they do not believe you are sincere! And I question it myself! Even your Suffete has refused to send reinforcements."

Hannibal stared expressionless at the table. "I suppose you all question me at this time."

"General, why did we stop when we were so close?" Gisgo said. "We could have had Rome by the throat. Instead, we have been fighting petty skirmishes...for years! The men are tired. I, too, am tired. As ashamed as I am to admit, General, I, too, question you."

Hannibal nodded. "And you, Ducarius. Surely, the Gaul are uneasy with my leadership."

Ducarius surveyed the men at the table until his gaze found Hannibal. "Yes, they are warriors. Warriors who have sworn loyalty to me. The same as I to you."

"Those are pretty words, Gaul," snorted Maharbal.

Ducarius snarled at the comment.

"It is time to return home," Hannibal whispered.

"Are you mad?" Maharbal said. "It is true that we have enjoyed the thrill of battle and the spoils that accompany it, but we were promised Rome!"

"My son Giscon will soon reach manhood. I have not seen him since he was born, ten years ago. And there is my beautiful wife, with whom I have never had the chance to share my love. They wait for me in Carthage."

Maharbal could not contain his disdain. "We have weakened the Romans! We swore to follow you! And now you have abandoned your men? It seems to be the Barca way."

Hannibal rose from his chair and drew his sword. Maharbal stood motionless, his eyes locked on his general. Hannibal gripped the hilt of his sword.

"The nightmares have never stopped. The dreams I had. The beautiful lands that I have only seen in books. The ones father would tell my brothers and me about. There are no beautiful lands. None! But I must learn to dream again, for the sake of my family."

"Hannibal?" Hanno felt Hannibal's pain.

"I have sent for Hasdrubal to help us secure a route home. This war is over." Hannibal threw his sword on the table. "I have lost the fire. I am going home." The men watched in utter silence as Hannibal headed toward the door. The poor soul had never healed from the death of Mago.

Maharbal would not let it end there, however. "The Romans have also lost many, Hannibal. They will not share your newfound interest in peace!"

Lilybaeum, Sicily—206 B.C.

Claudius Nero, a man with the crumpled face of a deep thinker, trailed Scipio down the hall leading to the main chamber in the fortress. They walked along the dim cavern, which was lit by flickering, fiery pits. As they passed guards along the path, their boot steps thumped down the hall.

"I grow tired of your approach, Proconsul," Scipio said. "I have been entrusted with the salvation of Rome, and I have limited time to secure it."

"Rest assured, Consul. Hasdrubal shall not step one foot into Rome. I swear."

Scipio paused for a moment and stared at Nero. "Do you?"

"Yes," Nero said after clearing his throat.

They continued on their trek.

"While I search for a foothold in Africa, you may be our last defense. What of Hannibal?"

"He has taken Tarentum."

"I already know that!"

"Governor Marcus is also dead," Nero added.

"That I did not know."

Nero smiled with excitement. "Oh yes, Consul. But he was unable to capture the citadel."

"Does he have the supplies to resist?" Scipio's eyes squinted, contemplating the resources available to Hannibal.

"Thanks to your guidance and skills, Consul, we continue to burn everything as we follow him. He has little or nothing to use. Sooner or later, he will be forced back to Apulia. What an excellent and decisive move on your part, Consul. I understand--"

Scipio silenced Nero mid-statement with a raise of his

palm. "I understand that I am an adroit individual. That is proven by having never been defeated as consul. Of course, I do not need you to tell me this. I was present every moment."

Nero cowered in embarrassment. "I meant no disrespect by--"

"Vanity has no place on the battlefield," Scipio said. The two men stopped before a wooden door as a Roman guard stepped aside, allowing his superiors to enter. "But that is restricted to the battlefield," said Scipio with a huge, sly grin.

Scipio and Nero entered a beautiful, sun-lit room, which was ornately decorated with exquisite Greco-Roman style furniture and sheer silk curtains. They were greeted by several African servants dressed in beautiful white robes—and by a beautiful young woman named Sophonisba. Sophonisba had dark, pearlescent skin and almond-shape, mesmerizing eyes. Her statuesque legs were accentuated by the fine, rare cloth that enveloped her curvaceous body from head to toe. She waited to be greeted.

Scipio and Nero each took a knee before the young woman, and Scipio gently kissed the cloth that dangled from her forearm. "Your mere presence, Queen Sophonisba, humbles even the gods."

Sophonisba broke away and gazed out the chamber window overlooking the Mediterranean. "My husband forewarned me that you were...how do they say in your land?...a nectar that entices only the snakes to drink."

Scipio looked at Nero. "Something like that, your Majesty. The Roman proverb, I mean."

Sophonisba turned and motioned to her servants to remove the first layer of cloth enveloping her. They did, revealing a little more of her magnificent figure. She approached Scipio slowly. "My husband also suggested that an alliance with Rome would better serve the Massaelylians."

"King Syphax is a very wise leader. Truly one destined to lead a people as great as yours."

Sophonisba smiled. "Syphax is very trusting as is my virulent son, Masinissa."

"You will be proud to know that he has served Rome splendidly and is greatly esteemed," responded Scipio.

Queen Sophonisba sauntered over to the window. "We will support you against the Carthaginians. I shall sail at daybreak to relay the news to my husband. We have agreed to commit soldiers and weapons on your behalf."

"Thank you," Scipio bowed.

There was a long pause before Sophonisba addressed the two Roman soldiers again. "That is all. You may leave now."

Scipio was a little caught off guard by her abruptness but eventually nodded to Nero to rise. Scipio's eyes were drawn to her once more before they departed the room.

23.

Near Ariminium, Etruria

Inside the nondescript tent stood a much older, bearded Hasdrubal, scanning a map of Etruria. He was frailer than normal, and his face was drawn inward from exhaustion. His journey to Africa, for which he had recruited several soldiers, proved to be more catastrophic than he had expected. Hannibal had now commanded him to move on to Etruria and secure safe passage to Carthage. Hasdrubal obeyed and led his infantry, cavalry and elephants along the same route through Gaul and Liguria that Hannibal had traversed twelve years earlier. Although he faced little resistance from the Gaul crossing the Alps, the elements were unforgiving. Upon his arrival in Etruria, Hasdrubal was greeted by Consul Marcus Livius and his legions.

"Commander, they have us surrounded!" screeched the Carthaginian officer who rushed in.

Hasdrubal closed his eyes in disappointment. "Any word from my brother?"

"No, Commander."

"I shall write another letter then." Hasdrubal stared vacantly into the distance.

"The forces, Sir? Shall I gather the forces?" the officer shouted, awaking Hasdrubal from his trance.

"Yes, form the battalions. Prepare messengers for immediate departure."

The officer put fist to chest and darted out the tent.

Hasdrubal sat at the table, picked up his quill and began to write another letter on a piece of parchment.

"Brother, I am here," Hasdrubal wrote. "The Romans somehow knew of my arrival and have my army trapped at Ariminium. They are four legions strong. My supplies are low and my men are weary from the trek through the Alps. This is my second message since my arrival. Once again, I need your help, Hannibal." As Hasdrubal continued to write, he remembered their times together, their days of playing in the sea as children. "If you have received the earlier message, then I shall see you soon." He remembered his first arrival at Hispania when they greeted each other with a brotherly embrace. "I hope Ba'al has watched over you. You are the only brother that I have left. I shall see you soon. Your brother, Hasdrubal."

Writing completed, Hasdrubal rolled up the scroll.

Apulia—203 B.C.

Hannibal sat at the head of the command chamber. He was out of his armor and dressed only in a toga. Synhus stood by his side, along with two guards. A Carthaginian soldier who carried a sack and a scroll ambled into the chamber. The battle-weary warrior collapsed to his knees before Hannibal. Hannibal rose and held him by the shoulders.

"Tell me of my brother!"

The soldier trembled as a tear trickled down his face. He did not lift his head. Hannibal grabbed the blood-soaked scroll and unrolled it. He took a moment to read it.

"He is in Ariminium! How strong is your army?"

Hannibal knelt beside the man.

"I was the only one who survived," the soldier muttered.

"The only one to survive? What of this letter?"

"I am not the messenger, General." The soldier swallowed his blood and saliva. "The Romans allowed me to live only so that I could deliver their message." The soldier handed Hannibal the sack.

Hannibal opened the sack, looking furtively at its contents. Horrified, he fell back with a sudden jolt. His chest heaved up and down and his eyes became gigantic, intense white ovals.

"It cannot be. No. No!"

Gisgo came to his aid. "General, what is it?"

Gisgo sprinted over to help him up, but Hannibal pushed him away and collapsed into his chair. Gisgo looked inside the bag. "Hasdrubal."

Hannibal wept upon his makeshift throne as Synhus placed his hand on his shoulder to comfort him. His sorrow welled up from within the depths of his soul, but his tears did not flow.

The soldier continued his message. "General, their message is...their message is that Consul Scipio shall meet you in Africa. Carthage shall belong to the last of the Barcas."

Suddenly, Hannibal came to his feet, taking a sword from one of his guards. Before Gisgo could stop him, Hannibal swung the blade and decapitated the soldier. His eyes as bright as the sun stared down the men in his court. He stood poised, ready to attack anyone who would be foolish enough to approach.

"He's going to attack Carthage." Hannibal had the look of a tiger ready to feed. He removed the top part of his robe, revealing his muscular, scarred frame. "Gisgo!"

Gisgo approached his commander. "Yes, General."

"Prepare our army for embarkment."

Utica, Africa

The spires and castles of Utica were ablaze as Roman soldiers gathered the native women and children and corralled them in an orderly fashion. Strewn along the cobblestone paths and along the walls of the fortified city walls were the bodies of dead African warriors, which were being looted by the Roman soldiers and then stacked into piles of death. Scipio galloped into the smoke on his mare, accompanied by several Roman tribunes. He acknowledged the soldiers' salutations and celebrations as he rode by.

The dingy, dimly lit prison chamber was a spacious room with several bondage chains bolted to the wall. The blood and skeletal remains of past prisoners littered the floor. As Scipio entered the chamber, fifteen Roman guards stood watch over their prisoners, Queen Sophonisba and her beloved husband King Syphax. King Syphax was a wide, aging man with a long, gray beard. His royal attire was tattered and dirty, a result of his failed efforts to escape. If it weren't for the chains on his wrists, the weak old man would have fallen to the ground. From the look on his face, Scipio deduced that Syphax had already been interrogated by his son Masinissa, the young man in dreadlocks and Roman armor.

"You are going to die, old man!" Masinissa grabbed his father by the throat. "Revenge is mine."

"You are a fool and no son of mine, traitor!" Syphax said with a snarl.

"You would not listen. You are to blame!" Masinissa

shook Syphax profusely. "It is time for you to die and for me to be king. Why can you not understand this?"

"All for the love of my wife, you betrayed me. The people will never follow you."

"They will follow me!" Masinissa drew his sword in anger, but Scipio held it back.

"Wait, Masinissa. You would kill your own father in cold blood? Where is this Hasdrubal?"

"He was killed in the invasion."

"I see." Scipio strolled over to Sophonisba. Her beauty had not faded, despite her being chained and dressed in ragged clothing like her husband. Scipio bowed before her.

"We would never betray our treaty, Roman." Sophonisba flashed a seductive, deceitful smile and looked at Scipio with her magical eyes. Scipio returned her gaze, upon which Sophonisba spat in his face. Scipio, did not lose his smile, but simply wiped the saliva on his cloak and sauntered over to Syphax.

"I would like to set you free, but how can I be certain that you will permit a woman to guide you in the future? You may decide to side with the Carthaginians again."

"Your tricks may work on my son and on the battlefield, Roman, but I know better than to trust you. We are African. Carthaginians are African. Rome is not African. You are not African," proclaimed the king.

Scipio sarcastically placed his hand on his heart. "Ouch." He strolled over to one of the guards. "Crucify them."

"Scipio wait! Sophonisba must not be harmed." Masinissa pleaded with Scipio.

Scipio moved within earshot. "Betrayal will be paid for with swift death."

"But you knew she would betray us," Masinissa said.

"We are to be married!"

Scipio pulled Masinissa over to the side. "You would marry a woman who betrayed your father?"

"I love her. We were supposed to be in each other's arms before he stole her from me."

Scipio sighed and then patted him on the shoulder. "I understand. Tonight, be together as husband and wife. I shall offer you a gift for the occasion." Scipio reached in his pouch and handed Masinissa a flask of clear liquid.

"What is this?" Masinissa studied the vial.

"Poison."

"Poison?"

"I am a reasonable man," Scipio said. "Tonight, be together. But at sunlight, the marriage shall be over."

"I will not--"

Before he could protest, Scipio glared at Masinissa. "It would be a shame for our two empires if we destroyed what we have worked so hard to build. Do you agree, King Masinissa?"

The unsheathing of Roman *gladii* captured Masinissa's attention. "I agree."

Scipio smiled once again. "Good." Scipio gazed over at Sophonisba, bowed and exited the room.

"I truly understand, King Masinissa."

Mediterranean Sea—202 B.C.

The waves of the Mediterranean crashed against the modest Carthaginian fleet. Maharbal stroked his steed to settle the beast. He wondered how long it would be before he tasted the mists of morning battle. Behind him, his

Numidians stood poised and ready. Gisgo and Ducarius stood in fully armor near the drums, observing their leader, Hannibal, who stood alone on the bow of the quinquereme as the drumbeat commanded the seamen below to row. Hannibal took a long look at the western coast of Lucania. As when he was a child leaving Carthage, he gazed longingly upon the horizon.

Carthage, Africa

The old guard has grown much older. Senator Cobo and Senator Bragibas strolled along a well-lit hall of the Suffete leading to a courtyard with an illustrious fountain. Hands behind their backs, they observed the clear skies above.

"The Romans are once again on our doorstep," Cobo said.

"Are they considering the peace treaty?" Bragibas said.

"They demand Sicily, Sardinia and Hispania...along with Corsica and Malta. In addition, our navy must be reduced. Most importantly, Rome has agreed to leave the Suffete intact."

"Perhaps we should wait for a response from General Barca."

"Hannibal?" Cobo faced his longtime political adversary. "He has caused us enough grief. Besides, I have proceeded with negotiations, and I believe that the terms are generous."

"You said that Rome has agreed to not harm the Suffete. How is that possible? They seem to have befriended you, Senator."

"Hardly." The two men stopped to admire the fountain. Cobo ran his wrinkled hand through the pristine, cool waters.

"Sacrifice, Senator. Are we to blame for a demagogue with his own agenda?"

Bragibas grabbed Cobo's wrist. "The Barca family has sacrificed much for Carthage. We cannot throw Hannibal Barca to the wolves."

"Why are you such a crusader, old friend? Thanks to the sacrifices of Hannibal, we have filled our coffers with riches beyond belief. One more offering will not do any harm."

"I will not let you abandon him. I stood by and let you do it once before. This time I will stop you." Bragibas released Cobo and stormed away.

"You cannot stop the inevitable, Senator. In time, you will see. By fighting me now you will only hurt yourself."

Bragibas stopped. "You are a pitiful, old man! I should have listened to Hamilcar many years ago. You are Rome herself!"

"I would be careful what I say, Senator. Such accusations are dangerous. Remember, no one man is greater than Carthage."

Bragibas departed in frustration.

24.

Zama, Africa

African serfs extinguished the smoldering campfires as the Carthaginian army of Gaul, Moors, Balearics, Iberians and Carthaginians donned their armor and armed themselves for the desert battle. The arid region had experienced fierce sandstorms in the last few weeks, and it was on this day that both armies prepared to engage one another. From within the command tent, Hannibal and Maharbal looked over a strategic map in preparation.

"Position your Numidians here," Hannibal said. "After the elephants complete their charge, engage their cavalry."

"It is good to fight in Africa again."

"This Scipio is unlike any consul in Rome. He is more intelligent and crafty. You must be as swift as the wind once the attack begins.

Gisgo barged in. "General, the scouts have returned!"

"I am aware of that, Gisgo."

"I speak of the ones that were captured by the Romans."

Hannibal was taken by surprise. "Were they mutilated or tortured?"

"No, they are in perfect health."

"What?" Hannibal turned his attention away from the map.

"He freed them with food and water to return here." Gisgo paused to regain his composure before continuing. "They told me that the Roman even gave them a tour of his camp!"

"Mad, like another leader I know," Maharbal said.

"He fights like me in theory and in practice." I want to meet this Scipio, Hannibal thought to himself. Once he had decided upon a strategy, he commanded Gisgo to return the scouts to the Roman camp and propose a meeting between Scipio and himself.

"That is foolish!" Maharbal said. "The Romans are not to be trusted. You of all people should know that."

"I have to speak with him. Gisgo, go!"

"Yes." Gisgo pounded his chest and vacated the tent.

"I will accompany you."

Hannibal placed his hand on the shoulders of the Numidian. "I would not go without you, my friend."

In the center of the vast, dry plain rests a small hill where Hannibal and Scipio would meet face to face for the first time. Scipio and a small force of legionnaires awaited the arrival of Hannibal and Maharbal accompanied by a few Numidian horsemen. At last, the two warriors faced each other on horseback. For a while, they studied each other's movements as the men in their respective parties regarded their adversaries with threatening stares.

"Two great nations come face to face once again."

"Yes, two great nations," Scipio responded sharply over the neighing of his mare.

"I am Hannibal Barca."

"I am aware of who you are. I am Publius Cornelius Scipio."

"The son of Cornelius Scipio," said Hannibal matter-of-factly.

"Do you not remember me, General?"

"I have faced many Romans in my years. You will have to forgive me if your appearance escapes me."

"You spared my father's life at Ticinus, along with mine."

Hannibal searched his memory. "And you took my brother Hasdrubal's life as gratitude."

"That was an unfortunate accident," Scipio said. "My officers can become aggressive, almost savage-like at times."

"Indeed, much like ours," Hannibal replied.

Scipio smirked, nodded and followed Hannibal as they steered their horses away from the men. The soldiers remained in their stern positions as the two generals took their positions at the edge of the hill, which overlooked the battlefield. They gazed out at the horizon.

Scipio began by stating the Roman demands. Hannibal, of course, saw things differently. "Leave Africa today, and Carthage will surrender Sicily, Hispania and Sardinia."

"We already have those terms with your Suffete. In fact, before you broke the treaty, Carthage owed Rome so much more."

"Rome broke the treaty, not Carthage!"

"Your fortunes as a leader are unsurpassed, General. Why should we fight this battle?" Scipio turned to Hannibal and awaited his response.

"Fortune? I can tell you that fortunes can change like the wind. Although I have defeated every army that has ever faced me, why do I feel like a beaten man? There is misfortune beyond the battlefield, Consul. So why should we fight this battle?" Hannibal struggled to understand the Roman's intentions. Part of Hannibal wanted to cut his throat, but part of him wanted to hear out the younger officer.

"We have fought long enough," Scipio replied. "I think that in another time we could have known each other on more civilized terms."

"That is exactly why we must engage in battle today. It must end with us. Alas, all the pain and dying must end with us." Hannibal leered at the Roman. "I had hoped that you would not accept the terms of treaty."

"Hoping I would not?"

"Yes, because treaties are superficial. They simply prolong the inevitable."

"Conquer or surrender." Scipio nodded with approval.

"It is the only way I can ensure that my son does not inherit my destiny as I did my father's."

"And I my father's." Scipio faced the battlefield once more. "It is an honor to battle you, General Barca."

Hannibal turned to Scipio. "Maybe when we have finished battling, we can share old war stories over wine."

"Yes, when it is over."

"May Ba'al watch over you." Hannibal put his fist to his chest. Scipio raised his palm in acknowledgement as Hannibal rode off.

Battle Of Zama

Only a few hundred yards separated the two massive forces. Hannibal commanded forty-five thousand men while Scipio led about thirty-six thousand.

Heavy drums played by muscle-bound African drummers signaled the warriors to form their lines. Mahouts mounted on eighty massive elephants stood ready at the front of Hannibal's division. Lightly armored troops of various nationalities were massed in the frontline, which was commanded by Hannibal. The second line, led by Gisgo, was comprised of more heavily armored soldiers, and the third was manned by hardened veterans from Etruria. Ducarius commanded them and stood in front of the line, covered in leather armor and facial paint. On their flanks were the Numidian and Iberian cavalries. Maharbal and Sosylos circled their men in preparation for battle.

The Roman velites, principes, triarii and hastati were amassed on the other side of the dry, grassy plain. The units were not formed into lines, but were separated from each other in a checkered pattern. Scipio rested upon his steed and scanned the field. He looked to his flanks where the Romans had positioned their own Numidians, who were led by Masinissa. Tribunes and trumpeters moved among the rest of the troops, shepherding them into their proper positions. Scipio prepared to give the final battle order.

Just inside the nondescript tent were Hannibal and Synhus. They looked into each other's eyes for a moment.

"You were right. You were always right," Hannibal said. "I should have listened to you all those years ago."

Synhus' mysterious expression had softened as it had over the years. "You listened to Ba'al. Now you must hear him again and abide by what he tells you. You are his son as was your father."

"I tried to find Imilce and Giscon in Carthage, but they never arrived from Hispania. If it ends here, tell them that they were always in my heart."

"I am an old man now. It is time that I take my leave," Synhus said.

Hannibal understood what he really meant. He knew that he would never see his surrogate father again. It saddened him deeply. Age and the loss of all of his brothers had consumed him, but at that moment he felt truly alone. "I will miss you." Hannibal embraced Synhus as a son does a father. He released him, grabbed his battle helm and left the tent.

Mounted on his steed, Hannibal headed up the frontline. He turned to Gisgo.

"Send the elephants."

Prodded by their mahouts, the animals trundled forward like boulders rolled downhill.

"Onward!" Scipio said.

The disciplined Roman infantry began their slow march forward, shields raised. The troops advanced toward the giant beasts in their checker formation, and then dispersed into a number of long columns with wide paths in between them.

The elephants crashed into several of the Roman soldiers, crushing some of them beneath their massive legs. Using their spears, the soldiers were able to direct many of the elephants toward the paths they had cleared so that the animals would run harmlessly past them. Some of the elephants were stabbed by the long spears, and in a panic, they turned and stampeded toward the Carthaginian lines. Chaos soon erupted in the frontline where several soldiers were crushed. However, the Carthaginian frontline was soon able to draw the elephants to their flanks and regain their bearings. The Moors and Iberians charged forward, shouting their battle cries.

The Roman infantry advanced to meet them, and the two forces clashed. The light-armored Carthaginian line held its ground for only a few minutes before it was driven back by the sharp *gladii* of the Romans. Many were cut down or in retreat toward Hannibal's second line.

"Second Line, hold your ground!" Hannibal said.

"Hold your ground, men!" echoed Gisgo.

Some in the retreating frontline attempted to slide their bloodied bodies past the forward-marching second line but to no avail; the advancing soldiers would not let them cross. Many simply collapsed from sheer exhaustion.

"Forward!" Gisgo said as he raised his hand.

The second line marched in quickstep as they approached the Roman infantry.

Scipio turned to a tribune. "Advance the cavalry!"

Masinissa and another Roman officer led the cavalry in a charge.

Hannibal unsheathed his sword and pointed it forward. Javelins extended, the Numidians erupted from their position. They were met by fellow Numidians in Masinissa's contingent. Spears pierced the bare-chested warriors, and soldiers on both sides were felled from their mounts. Many of the fallen riders were trampled by the heavy hooves of the horses that circled around them.

"Masinissa, you traitor!" Maharbal said. Masinissa heard the challenge and rode toward Maharbal.

Sosylos's men engaged the Roman cavalry, filling the battlefield with the sound of clashing swords and the wails of men whose flesh was being hacked from their hapless bodies.

"Prepare to engage!" Hannibal dismounted his horse and unsheathed a second sword to complement the one already in his hand.

The Carthaginian second line was overwhelmed. Many began retreating to the third line, but most had already been mortally wounded by the heavily armored hastati. Among them was Gisgo, who was lying on the ground, covered in blood, trying to lift his body from the carnage above him. The Roman soldiers were fatigued but continued to march forward.

The soldiers of the Carthaginian third line refused to allow the retreating second line to pass, just as they had turned away the troops fleeing the frontline. The third line charged forward in full battle cry, Hannibal leading the assault.

"Prepare to flank!" Hannibal said.

The approaching Romans began to fan out and form a single line. This caught Hannibal by surprise.

"Hold your places! Never backward, only forward!" Scipio said.

The two forces clashed. Weapons sliced and gutted. Carthaginian swords and axes bounced off Roman shields, but several found their targets on the limbs of the Roman legionnaires.

While their cavalries exchanged deathblows, Masinissa and Maharbal circled each other on their horses, exchanging parries with their spears.

"No wonder you fight with the Romans. The weak relying on the weaker!" Maharbal taunted Masinissa, who was almost out of breath.

"It is you who are fighting for the wrong army!" retorted Masinissa.

Maharbal deflected Masinissa's jab and speared Masinissa in the back. Masinissa grunted in agony as blood flowed from the wound.

"Yes! Let's battle!" Maharbal gloated.

Sosylos fought desperately to protect himself from the Romans surrounding him. He swung his broadsword through the air, failing to connect with his targets. In the distance, he could see some of his horsemen retreating. "Cowards! Fight! We must fight!" Sosylos said right before a *pilum* whistled through the air and penetrated his abdomen. Sosylos groaned and dropped his weapon. He lost consciousness and fell from his horse.

Hannibal was fighting with the ferocity he had when he first entered Etruria. He twirled his two blades with great ferocity, slashing any Roman who came near him. "Fight until the cavalry arrives! They are growing weary. We have them!" he cried.

Scipio dismounted and unsheathed his *gladius*. A Gallic soldier went on the assault. Scipio evaded the battle-ax and ended the man's life with an upward swing.

"Where is my cavalry?" Scipio shouted.

The Numidians continued their melee, and bodies littered their battlefield. Though he was growing tired, Maharbal continued his assault on Masinissa. In a thorough manner, he had beaten his fellow Numidian. As he was removing Masinissa from his mount, he was struck in the leg by a spear. Maharbal dislodged the weapon and gritted his teeth to overcome the pain.

"Ah, victory feels good, does it not?" said Maharbal as he was stabbed in the back by another spear. He coughed up blood. Another projectile pierced his chest. Once he was on the ground, passing enemy Numidian riders launched their weapons into his lifeless body.

An attacking Roman had slashed Hannibal in the leg, but he soon recovered and lodged his sword into his assailant's neck. He dropped one sword and fell to one knee. As another legionnaire ran at him, he used the man's momentum to flip him over his shoulder. Hannibal then ended the prone man's life with a sharp stab in his chest. Out of breath and in pain, Hannibal observed the battle around him. His men were falling. The soldiers that had served him for so many years were dying before his eyes. Some were in a complete panic as the Roman cavalries stampeded through the Carthaginian ranks.

Hannibal heard footsteps behind him. He spun around and swung his weapon, which was immediately blocked by Ducarius's sword.

"General, you must leave the battlefield!" Ducarius pleaded.

Several Gaul surrounded Hannibal and defended him.

"Where am I going to go? This is my home!" Hannibal searched his surroundings. "Maharbal..."

"He's dead!" Ducarius said.

Hannibal fell to his knees. "Maharbal is dead. Maharbal cannot die."

"Gisgo, Sosylos...they are all dead! We have to retreat, General!"

At sunset, a pride of lions lined the sandy hills overlooking epic battlefield. The cubs played with each other while the lionesses surveyed the horizon for prey. The field was strewn with dead bodies as far as the eye could see. Romans, Carthaginians, Gaul, Iberians, Moors, Celtiberians, and others lay motionless in the dry, grassy field. Serfs picked through the bodies for valuables as Roman legionnaires carried away their dead for burial.

Scipio stood on the battlefield. The sand which had been kicked up by a strong west wind swirled around him. He was bloodstained from battle. Grime covered his face. He scanned the horizon and the thousands dead before him. Scipio unsheathed his sword, took a knee in the sand and laid his sword down. He looked to the sky in order to face the gods.

"Now, it is over."

25.

Carthage, Africa—190 B.C.

The interior of the cold Suffete building had not changed but Hannibal had. Alone he stood before the senators, dressed in a flowing white toga. He was graying and years of torment showed on his face. His carriage had lost its confident swagger.

The familiar faces of the Suffete had not changed either. But, alas, Bragibas was no longer among them. Senator Cobo stood at the head of the panel, some ten feet above Hannibal.

"The Roman Senate demands your surrender for war crimes against them. It pains me to level these charges now, considering the civic services you have performed since your retirement from military service."

"What crimes have I committed?" Hannibal shouted at the elderly senator.

"Murder, rape, pillaging and the destruction of the land surrounding Rome."

"I see."

"We are not able to protect you, General Barca," Cobo said. "The vote was overwhelmingly against you. Only Senator Bragibas voted in your favor, but unfortunately he is no longer with us. Therefore, the Suffete hereby banishes Hannibal Barca and his entire bloodline from the walls of Carthage. You are to leave immediately."

"My son is Carthaginian. You cannot keep him from his true home."

"Given that this imaginary son of yours has never stepped one foot into Carthage, we will make an exception for him."

"It is still not over," Hannibal insisted.

"Pardon, General Barca? I could not hear you."

"I said that it is still not over!"

"Yes, it is truly over. We are finished."

"They will keep coming!"

"We are finished, General." Cobo slammed both palms on the podium.

"Rome wants Carthage. That is why they still are hunting me today. I am the last thorn in their side."

"Get the guards! The man has gone mad."

"Whatever happens, I must continue to oppose Rome at all costs." Hannibal then moved closer to their high podiums. "I have something to say."

Two huge Carthaginian guards entered the room.

"Guards, take that man away from here!"

The two guards approached Hannibal. But when the former general faced them, they stopped in their tracks, showing him the respect to which a man of his stature was entitled.

"I have something to say," Hannibal said.

The two guards bowed before Hannibal and backed away.

"Guards, I said..." Cobo realized further commands were wasted words.

Hannibal faced the Suffete. "The Barca family has given everything to Carthage. We have nothing left, only love for Carthage. I will continue to make war on Rome until it is no longer a threat to Carthage. And if you stand in my way, I will make war on the Suffete."

"Is that a threat?" Cobo rose from his chair. "How dare you attack those who have given you so much support."

"And my son will know of your treachery," continued Hannibal. "You have had the pleasure of having a Barca as an ally. Now you will know how it feels to have a Barca as your enemy."

Hannibal walked out of the room with resolve to the disapproving grumbles of the Suffete.

Bithynia, Asia Minor—182 B.C.

Hannibal smashed the cup on the floor.
"My love and hate are one."
"I must take you to Rome. I will protect you." Scipio smiled.
"Scipio?"
"Yes?"
"Let an old man die in peace."

Hannibal grinned one last time before his eyes glazed over and he stopped breathing. Scipio placed his hand on Hannibal's shoulder. "Hannibal?" Scipio soon realized that Hannibal had died and was saddened. He walked over and picked up the cup that Hannibal was drinking from and sniffed it. "Poison."

Scipio chuckled. The Carthaginian would not be taken on some other's terms, Scipio thought to himself. Even in death, Hannibal had been able to best another Roman consul. Upon regaining control of his laughter, he bid his friend an emotional farewell. Scipio reached over to Hannibal and closed the general's eyes.

"Today, I rejoice. At least it is over for you, my friend." Scipio stood and adjusted his cape while staring at Hannibal. He noticed the scroll that Hannibal had in hand their entire conversation. Scipio removed it from Hannibal's grasp and examined the parchment. Upon it was the sketch of the lion and river from Hannibal's dream, painted by Hasdrubal many years ago. Scipio leaned down and placed the crumpled, bloodstained painting on Hannibal's chest.

"May Ba'al watch over you."

Epilogue

Young Hannibal waded over the riverbank and prayed to Ba'al to watch over him. The mist became a thick, white, organic cloud, almost suffocating him. He did not see the bottom through the vapor but heard heavy splashing near his feet. Hannibal gazed once more at the blood that covered his tiny hands and watched them dry and crack. Pendulous dollops of red slowly fell to the earth. He did not turn to face it, but Hannibal felt the heavy paws of the beast trampling the dead leaves that littered the muddy coast. Still, he waited for the pain to begin. If he were to die, he preferred slashing and gnawing to the grim fate that awaited him in the river.

But the lion did not pounce nor did it slash. It found its way to Hannibal and sat beside him while looking over the horizon. Within its jaws hung the four slain cubs that Hannibal had seen once before. The lion twirled its head as the cubs danced limply from side to side. Hannibal watched in sadness as the proud lion dropped the small cubs into the mist. Four splashes confirmed the descendent of the brood, and the bereaved father summoned a last roar.

"Forgive me," whispered Hannibal as he faced the lion.

The lion stood on all fours once more and circled Hannibal. His bristly fur rubbed up against Hannibal's leg. The wild beast's back stood as high as Hannibal, and its massive jaws could swallow the boy without chewing.

Yet Hannibal was no longer afraid. He now regarded the lion with a certain sense of familiarity. At that moment, he knew that the animal was not the bloodthirsty beast he imagined. He was his guardian in this horrific world. He served as a warning to stop the path of destruction. Once Hannibal understood this, his heart began to ache and regret snatched him by the throat. He had the frame of a child and the memories of a battle-scarred old man. His knees fell to the sticky mud and he extended his hand, hoping that the lion would enter his embrace.

"Father?"

Hannibal's watery eyes beckoned the lion to come near. He did. He licked the face of the warrior child, and his fierce eyes focused on Hannibal's smile. Hannibal knew the lion was Hamilcar, and he embraced the lion, burying his face in the mane.

"I know we have to go." Hannibal could hear the lion's thoughts as clear as if he had spoken them. "Yes, I want to see my brothers again."

Side by side, they entered the mist, disappearing into the void. Hannibal enjoyed the peace that had eluded him for so long.

He dreamed no more.

For Oriana

Here's a special sneak preview

of

The Lion's Brood

The Mercenary War

Coming in January 2011

As the battle for
Mediterranean dominance
continues...

Carthage—180 BC

With the coastal city on the Mediterranean nestled in the background, a lone figure on horseback made his way over the grassy plains, leaving Carthage in the distance. A portentous cloak and hood hid his identity from anyone brave enough to inquire. Slowly, the horse galloped along a narrow path, lined with decrepit and weathered stone dwellings. Many were homes and farmland abandoned many years ago. He hears only the whistling of the wind.

Several children scurried up to the path, causing the rider's horse to neigh, its nostrils aquiver with discontent. The children wore shredded tunics, and soil covered their limbs. Keeping up with the trotting steed, they attempted to sell several items in their possession to the traveler—rusty shields, dented helmets, moldy leather armor.

"One silver piece could feed my family, Sir!"

"This very valuable, Sir. But it is yours for just a little kindness!"

"This is from the war, used by General Barca himself in Etruria!"

The rider stopped. The children came to an abrupt halt. They waited patiently, silent with their faces pointed to the man in the sky. The man reached into his dark cloak and pulled out a pouch that jingled when he tossed it to the feet of the children. Like wild dogs, the forgotten children fought over the sack, flinging silver coins in all directions. The cloaked figure nudged the horse's midsection with the heels of his goatskin sandals and galloped ahead.

The dark rider reached the coast of the Mediterranean where on the cliff ahead sat the silhouette of a stone dwelling of moderate size. He stopped and removed his hood to reveal his bronze complexion, dark bushy hair tied in the back, and eyes that were as intense as they were troubled. He scanned the acres of land that surrounded the home. The field was unkempt and relics of tilling equipment littered the dry land.

The man dismounted and approached the weathered estate. There were cracks in the stone, and weeds sprouted from their crevices. As he climbed the stairs leading to the main entrance, one of the wooden window covers creaked back and forth with a sudden gust of wind.

He pounded the steel knocker on the door and waited for a moment. With no response, he leaned forward, trying to peak inside the crack of the six-inch square peep door.

The peep door slid open and a woman's face appeared, startling him.

"Yes?"

The man cleared his throat and gathered himself. "I am here as a representative of the Treasury. I have been tasked to recover the personal property of the Barca name in accordance with Carthaginian law."

"There are no more Barcas," the lady responded with hesitation.

"Yes, we are aware of such facts. Nevertheless, acquiring said items must be attained."

The door was unlocked and swung open to reveal a middle-aged woman holding a torch in a defensive posture. A thick robe covered her petite, African frame.

"Nothing is left since Lady Nara died five years ago."

"Who are you?" The man said as he stepped inside.

"I am Lorali. I served the Barca family for many years. The home was bequeathed to me upon her death."

"I understand. There are other possessions that still remain, are there not?"

"Most were taken by Lord Hannibal before leaving Carthage."

"What of his brothers?"

"They never returned from the war. Their spirits must dwell with Ba'al. Perhaps his sister still lives, but she has not been seen outside of Tunis, fearing Roman retribution. Alas, the vexation for Lady Nara was unbearable. Why must they take more?"

"I have not an answer." The man lowered his head in disappointment and began to depart. "Thank you."

"Wait!"

He stopped.

"There is something," she added.

Lorali led the man through the stark home with only the torch illuminating the dark passage.

"What of your husband?"

"He passed into the next world. It has made it difficult to maintain things up to standards."

"How are you able to eat? To live?" the man said while brushing cobwebs out of his path.

They stopped at a chamber door.

"This has always been my home." Lorali placed a hand on the large wooden door's bronze handle. "I could never leave."

The bedroom door creaked open. Before entering, Lorali used the torch to light the lamp near the entrance. Light revealed bedding, several intricate sculptures and a chest at the foot of the bed.

"Is this the private chamber of Hamilcar and Nara?"

"I have not entered this room since she left." A tear trickled down her face. "I could never have allowed myself to bear the sadness...until this moment."

"May Ba'al shine upon you for your kindness."

Lorali's eyes narrowed. "It is more than kindness, Sir. It is fear. There are times that I know the spirits of the dead still claim this place as their home."

He gave the woman a quick glance and entered the room. The man espied the entire room until his gaze found a painting of Nara hanging on the north wall.

"What am I searching for?" He shouted to the lady behind him.

Lorali remained outside the room with her eyes wide open. "The chest. Lady Nara would keep the letters of Lord Hamilcar and read them at night, alone. They may be of little value to you."

The man sat on the bedding and slowly lifted the lid of the chest. Inside, he saw several unrolled scrolls, tied together with thin string. There was also a green fist-size stone beside the multitude of letters.

"There are those who search for answers to many questions," the man said while his hand sifted through the papers. "These may be of great value."

"I shall leave you to your business, Sir."

"Wait. Can you tell me of their son, Hannibal?"

"He was a fiery child, but I am unable to tell you anymore. He left home very young, and when he returned, he said very little to anyone."

The man nodded and Lorali quietly dismissed herself.

He took the stack of letters from the chest and untied the string meticulously. The ink was faded, but he was still able to make out the Phoenician letters. He faced the burning lamp, ensuring the best possible light for reading, and read the first letter.

Nara, my love, what a fool I was to leave you behind. If I could see your beautiful eyes once more, then I would be able to die without regret. So, I must live.

War is not meant for men. It is for beasts that have a cold heart and an unforgiving mind. Have I become such a beast? Am I capable? Not having witnessed your beauty in so many moons, I know that war is not in my heart.

Cape Ecnomus, Mediterranean Sea—256 BC

Like sharp blades, the armada of Carthaginian triremes sliced through the crashing waves. Row after row of long paddles protruding from the belly of the ships moved in unison to the drumbeats coming from the huge bare-chested Libyan drummers pounding away below deck.

Many of the men have fought for many years and have left their families and homes behind. Many fight for riches only or the utter hatred of Rome.

Officers shouted orders to the many seamen maintaining the large square sails of each vessel. Seamen from various lands—Libyans, Numidians, Iberians and Celts—scurried around the deck, ensuring the trireme maintained its course.

Whatever their reason, they fight with such fierceness, beyond what I have ever seen. There is much bloodshed and death. More than I would ever desire to fall upon your eyes.

On one of the larger quinqueremes stood Commander Bragibas in full plate armor with a stare that sees more than what he is revealing. He was a big man and a seasoned officer in the Carthaginian ranks. With a square jaw, he looked ahead as his men carried out their pre-battle duties.

Within the hull of the ship, in a damp small room lit by only a window portal sat Hamilcar Barca, a young officer with a heavy brow. He was adorned in bronze plate armor. As he sat on the floor, he composed the final words of Nara's letter. The instruments he used, cloth, a seagull's quill and a small flask octopus ink, slid back and forth from the motion of the ship. The heavy drums echoed in the background.

Sicily is almost equal in beauty to Carthage. When the war is over, we shall view it together. Bostar is as foolish as ever. He seems to never be afraid. Part of me envies his fortitude. He is a good friend.
I miss you. May Ba'al shine upon you.
Your Love,
Hamilcar.

Just as Hamilcar finished writing, the quill was snatched from his hand.

Hamilcar leaped up and faced the older Bostar. His friend's dark complexion and chiseled face never matched the wily expression of his boon companion and compatriot, in Hamilcar's opinion. Dressed in plate armor as well, Bostar twirled the quill while holding a small flask of wine in the other hand. As usual, he did it with a grin.

"Writing a lover on duty?"

"Give that back! I will not climb another mast to get another!"

"Perhaps you would. You would climb the highest towers for your love, Nara."

Hamilcar attempted to snatch the quill, but Bostar pulled back in time.

"Jealousy will one day be your downfall, Bostar."

"Jealousy?"

"Yes, jealousy."

"Of you? A lion jealous of the sheep?"

Hamilcar became irritated and hurled himself at Bostar, who laughingly shoved the smaller Hamilcar away and held the quill near the open window portal. He taunted the distraught Hamilcar.

"What is the worth of your transgression?"

"Officers do not behave in such a manner, you droll. But over the years, I have learned much from you, my friend of so many years." Hamilcar unfolded his fist and revealed the flask that once belonged to Bostar. He did it with a grin.

Bostar was shocked to see his empty palm.

"You are a devious man, Hamilcar Barca."

"How devious am I? Would you like to find out?"

Hamilcar simulated tipping the flask over.

"Agreed."

Bostar accepted defeat, and they carefully exchange the items. Hamilcar placed the quill within a seam of the tunic under his armor.

"Officers do not indulge in grog before a battle."

Bostar drank from the flask. "You should learn to indulge, my friend. It is your last voyage."

Hamilcar smiled. "That it is."

"Any man that volunteers for military service in the name of love is foolish."

"My mother would not approve of our union, so I claimed my rite as a man."

"What a fool. Try not to die on your last campaign, will you?"

The heavy drums above deck increased tempo, which signaled to the young officers that the battle was at hand. Bostar and Hamilcar's eyes connected, and they sprinted out of the cabin.

Once they reached the top, the two men took notice of the Roman quinqueremes approaching the Carthaginian armada. At the head of the Roman fleet were two large hexereis (ships with six banks of oars) with the rest following in a spearhead formation. Behind them was the south coast of Sicily.

"There are so many." Hamilcar faced Bostar. "How are they able to have so many ships?"

"I do not know," Bostar whispered as he walked away.

The seamen dropped sail.

"Officers!" Bragibas stood on the upper deck.

Hamilcar, Bostar and four other Carthaginian officers hurried up the wooden stairs to where Bragibas stood. Before reaching the foot of the stairs, Hamilcar snagged a small man wearing only a tunic and handed him the scroll letter he was writing to Nara. The man nodded and continued on. Hamilcar reached the others as Bragibas used his sword as a pointer on the deck. He shouted over the drumbeat.

"Admiral Hamilcar shall draw their center outward!

Thus, enabling our squadron and Commander Hanno's squadron to engage their flanks! Since we're near coastal waters, fog is expected. However, it may be to our advantage." Bragibas looks up for a brief moment and raises one eyebrow before continuing. "Once their center has passed, we shall circle back to assist the admiral and crush their main push! Afterward, we will finish their remaining two squadrons and transports!"

"The admiral and I share the same name," Hamilcar whispered to Bostar with a proud smile.

"We are not exactly known for original thought when it comes to naming our offspring," Bostar replied.

Bragibas continued. "Remember to remain in your positions! Under no circumstances are you to leave your section of the ship undefended! Maintain that same discipline in your men! Are there any questions?"

The officers shook their heads.

"Good." Bragibas sheathed his sword. "May Ba'al shine upon us, and may Romans lie at our feet!"

The officers cheered and put their fist to their chest in salutation. They scattered to their respective sections.

Bostar grabbed Hamilcar's arm. He beamed with excitement.

"Till we meet at the bottom of the sea!"

Hamilcar smiled. "The sea is not large enough for us both!"

They clasped hands, embraced and push each other away in the spirit of the moment.

The Roman command ship carved its way through the sea. The massive hexereis was covered with Roman legionnaires, standing in formation and dressed in full armor and shields. On the prow of the vessel, as with all the ships in the fleet, was the *Corvus*—a 24-foot high pole with a pulley release system attached to a 36-foot long gangway with a long iron spike underneath at its tip. The ship led the 200-ship fleet and moved at top speeds with the power of the rowers below deck—the tantara of conches commanding the motion.

Observing the approaching Carthaginian ships from the ship's prow was Marcus Atilius Regulus with fierce eyes poking through his bronze helmet. He flung his crimson cape back to raise his palm in salutation to the approaching tribune.

"The boarding parties are assembled, Consul."

"Very well. Let us hope that Consul Vulso is as prepared."

"By your command."

The tribune saluted and departed.

Regulus whispered a prayer to Neptune as the fog grew thicker and the sun disappeared. He knew the Carthaginian vessels outnumbered his fleet by at least a hundred ships. Nevertheless, confidence was his strong point, and Regulus wanted victory at all costs, even if it required the entire Roman fleet plummeting to the bottom of the sea. I must rely on my experience, he thought. Regulus had spent the last eight of his thirty-year existence at sea, battling the Carthaginians for control of the *Mare Internum*. He knew his enemy all too well.

Hamilcar donned his helmet as he watched the middle of his fleet slow down and row in reverse. On the starboard side, several of the Roman ships two hundred feet away, led by Regulus' vessel, drifted past. Through the dense fog,

Hamilcar could see the silhouettes of Roman marines moving toward the prow of their ships.

"Steady men." Hamilcar took a deep breath scanned the seamen of various races around him. Some of them returned nervous nods of reassurance while others snarled at the anticipation of battle.

Once the middle of the Roman fleet passed, the ships towing supply vessels were exposed to Bragibas and the Carthaginians. The Carthaginian warships shifted direction toward the supply vessels and moved closer. The rowers below doubled their row speed. Hamilcar watched as the Roman warships release the supply ships by severing the lines connected. Bragibas startled him.

"Prepare for ramming!"

The seamen, including Hamilcar, secured themselves to any stationary object they could grab.

The Roman vessels began rotating to engage, but the Carthaginian ships were a mere 50 feet away before the Roman vessels could negotiate their turn. Their delay sealed their fate.

As the Roman ships floated closer, Hamilcar took one more deep breath as he espied several of the Roman seamen sprinting to their starboard side and leaping into the sea, the fortunate ones.

The powerful, iron-clad ram at the base of the Carthaginian warship's prow found its mark.

Crash!

Hamilcar was unable to maintain his balance, many of his comrades as well, and rolled to the deck. He regained his footing right after the sudden jolt and peered over the ship's railing. He watched as the Roman ship they engaged splintered at the hull. Water poured into its gaping belly and

Roman seaman fell into the sea—some covered in blood from the wreck.

The Carthaginians rejoiced as several of the seaman propelled short spears at the Romans attempting to swim below. Some of the projectiles connected, soon transforming the sea to crimson. Bragibas smiled from his command post, but his gratification soon dissipated.

"Roman trireme on our port!" an Iberian officer said to Bragibas.

The fog blinded the commander's specious decision to not check the ship's perimeter before all-out attack. Consequently, a Roman trireme was able to circumvent the Carthaginian main assault and circle to within thirty yards of the quinquereme's port. The ships moved parallel to each other, coasting in opposite directions with only a white mist separating them.

"Full reverse!" Bragibas ordered.

Hamilcar dashed to the opposite side of the deck, followed by the group of seamen under his command. His heartbeat raced, and his face became cold and damp. Hamilcar squinted to get a clearer view of the approaching enemy covered in fog. The Roman ship floated closer, slowly reducing the distance between both vessels.

"What are they planning to do, Sir?" a young seaman behind Hamilcar said.

"To fight," Hamilcar said without taking his sight off the shadowy behemoth portside. "Do not worry. You have been trained properly." He looked over his shoulder and saw the fear in the lad's eyes. "Stay close to me, and you will be fine."

The young seaman nodded.

Those reassuring words benefited Hamilcar as well. He

had been in two sea battles since joining the Carthaginian navy, but he had never engaged in hand-to-hand combat. However, he was an excellent swordsman. A cold chill rushed through his frame with the realization that he may have lived his last day. He looked to his right and saw Bostar at the other end of the ship staring his direction. In his usual way, Bostar's eyes and mouth widened to their fullest. He flexed his chest and biceps like a wild beast claiming its territory. Then he laughed, although Hamilcar could not hear it. Expressionless, Hamilcar took a deep breath, nodded to his friend in the distance and continued gazing at the approaching warship.

To be continued...